COPYRIGH

"There are two equal and opposite errors into which our race can fall about the devils. One is to disbelieve in their existence. The other is to believe, and to feel an excessive and unhealthy interest in them. They themselves are equally pleased by both errors and hail a materialist or a magician with the same delight."

– C. S. LEWIS (The Screwtape Letters)

Holy Ghost Exorcist

I certainly do wear a lot of hats in life. Whereas I have become somewhat notable as an author of extremely violent and visceral horror stories under this pen name of B. L. Blankenship, it is also a well-known fact that I'm a preacher. It is something that I've been very open about in interviews and within my fictional books as well. As a minister, I personally know several preachers who genuinely are following the leading of the Holy Ghost and are thereby working in deliverance ministry. While everything is being done in an appropriate, orthodox, and respectable way – within the specific churches that I am thinking of – they've faced a lot of combativeness and contention. The way the story goes in this fictional book could easily be any one of them – and has, in essence, been many of them. It's extremely realistic, so much so that Holy Ghost Exorcist is applicable for a television series, mini-series, or movie – in which medium it'd likely be classified as a drama, whereas within literature I've chosen to categorize it as Southern Gothic. This book is dedicated to all of those ministries, both big-time, like Apostle Greg Locke, Apostle Alexander Pagani, Dr. Bob Larson, Apostle Jennifer LeClaire, Pastor Mike Signorelli, Rev. Isaiah Saldivar, Pastor Vlad Savchuk, the late Father Gabriel Amorth, the late Dr. Kenneth Hagin, the late Rev. Win Worley, Pastor Rev. John Ramirez, and Pastor Ryan LeStrange; as well as the countless other unnamed men and women who've labored – stormed the gates of Hell and set the captives free by adhering to the totality of the Great Commission, which also entails the casting out of demons.

"Afterward he appeared unto the eleven as they sat at meat, and upbraided them with their unbelief and hardness of heart, because they believed not them which had seen him after he was risen. And he said unto them, Go ye into all the world, and preach the gospel to every creature. He that believeth and is baptized shall be saved; but he that believeth not shall be damned. And these signs shall follow them that believe; In my name shall they cast out devils; they shall speak with new tongues; They shall take up serpents; and if they drink any deadly thing, it shall not hurt them; they shall lay hands on the sick, and they shall recover. So then after the Lord had spoken unto them, he was received up into heaven, and sat on the right hand of God. And they went forth, and preached every where, the Lord working with them, and confirming the word with signs following. Amen." – MARK 16:14-20 KJV

I feel such humility at the faithfulness of some. There are people on the mission field in foreign lands who suffer real persecution; there are people such as these who are afflicted for helping the hurting. I used to feel so invincible. I've studied such dark things, and how

I've touched the darkness. I only began to feel vulnerable when it touched me back. This did come with some benefit as it opened my eyes. I went down a rabbit trail that caused me to discover Dr. Derick Prince and to become reacquainted with my teenage ministerial hero, Dr. Bob Larson. My hopes are that perhaps this book will do more than just entertain and captivate the readers. Perhaps it will make these people's reality easier in this aspect, anyway. GOD knows that I have prayed so much more for so many of them that they couldn't even imagine it.

When Pastor Greg Locke was talking all of his cessationist nonsense years ago – and breaking my heart like Samuel's was broken when the people wanted a king – I'd pray that GOD would open his eyes and use me to bring glory to His name, and He did. Today, Apostle Greg Locke has a lot of humility that most people just don't see. That man gives all for the cause of Christ. He's suffered a lot of things for the name of Jesus. I'm very proud of all of the positive changes that I've personally witnessed men like him as well as others making. While in his past he was known for a lot of controversial stuff, politics, and everything – he's actually made vast strides to put that behind him – taking down viral videos and so forth. Sadly, he still has an amassment of detractors. So many of us in ministry – I mean real ministry, not motivational speaking for a paycheck – we do what we do because we genuinely love The LORD and people. As odd as it might seem to want this from a

fiction book, I hope this book touches all of these real, true-blue, holdout-for-GOD ministries that practice deliverance: all of them, somehow, in some way…

Wow! This book kind of hangs in the balances of two very different and polarizing worlds. As a minister who believes in the power, working, and gifts of GOD – both through a strong theological knowledge and personal experience that perfectly backs up that knowledge on one hand, and as someone who has written violent horror novels comparable to the level of the sinful depravity conveyed in Jack Ketchum books, there is this. As my readers know – or at least the ones who read the acknowledgements, introductions, postscripts, and so forth – while my sales continue to climb, and certain upcoming anthologies look to republish some of my short stories – I announced some time back that it was my intention to step back from writing that sort of thing. With that being said, there are a great many people within the literary world of horror who've been kind to me. It has likewise been my pleasure partnering with them in various anthologies.

Besides that otherwise unnamed throng of people within the books that I've been in, festivals that I've attended, author interviews that I've had, and so forth – I am likewise extremely appreciative of my editor. She's made my life much easier, and I count working with her as both a blessing and privilege. I'm one of those people who is resistant to change. I'm a nester. Having an editor who I didn't know scared me. She has been nothing but wonderful. She's not done anything that changed my writing tone/voice. Frankly, she's a blessing who was introduced to me by extreme horror author – and all around sweetheart – Megan Stockton.

More than anyone else, I'm thankful to GOD. I'm thankful for the gifts that He has given me within music, art, and literature. They give me peace. Creating things makes me happy. I know that some people feel joy at watching a ballgame, or catching a fish. For me, it's writing, recording, and producing a song; or writing and publishing a book – things like that. It's like there is a sort of creativity in me that flows out of me like water. It makes me feel like I'm being productive and I enjoy doing it.

Far too many people to account for have told me how my cover art has notably been on a higher level than most indie books. Wendy Saber Core is largely to blame for that. Wendy generally works in two genres – horror and metal. I actually teamed up with Wendy on this cover as well.

Perhaps there is much more that could be said here. As I've stated numerous times before, all of the things that are written before the chapters of a fiction book feel more difficult to me than writing the actual story. Perhaps it is because I am trying to be brief. Brevity does not suit me. And while some religious person may act as though that is a bad thing – I feel that it is evident

to anyone of discernment that anything worth saying is worth saying well.

Besides all of that, though, I would like to additionally say thank you to people who actually go on Amazon, Goodreads, Barnes & Noble, Books-A-Million, Walmart, and other websites where my books are sold and take the time to review them. By this I do not mean merely leaving 1-5 stars – I mean, explaining why the story struck you the way that it did. It seems helpful in the way that it may cause others who could enjoy that book to read it while deterring those who might not to stay away. At any rate, it is appreciated. Like art, literature too is subjective.

Quite literally, on the day that I finished writing the last chapter of this book and began writing the introduction, a friend and fellow author contacted me, saying that he was driving to a funeral of the fifth person to die of suicide this year within the same family. In response, I told him that suicide is a very real demonic spirit. Likewise, there are generational curses that can take hold of people. It seemed to me as more than just a coincidence that so many people from the same family took their own lives in the same exact barn. I offered for him to give his friend my contact information – telling him that there really is freedom from that sort of thing.

Whereas it would be unimaginably ignorant to think that GOD receives anyone's prayers the same, He does still hear prayers and answer them. The Bible teaches that the double-minded hypocrite's prayer is prayed in vain. Likewise, the faithless prayer is to no effect. There are demonic forces who can only come out through prayer and fasting.

Those who truly know me know I am a man of extremes. After stepping down from my first pastorate at 21, I grieved terribly, shaved my beloved thick head of hair in mourning as unto the LORD and went on a 40-day fast – which I would not recommend to anyone unless they were completely sincere, sold out to GOD, and felt led to do so by the Holy Spirit. It was torturous, and you begin to have what is best described as manic-depressive hallucinations after the 21st day. During that fast, I only drank water, juice, and took holy Communion once a day. Remarkably, the mind-numbing headaches that I've gotten during long fasts can be knocked out with a tall, cold glass of orange juice. There's a science behind it somewhere – I imagine. But then, I've gone on a lot of fasts. I've been on 1, 3, 7, 14, and 21 days, generally, with pretty well the same terms as I stated for the 40 – more times that I can even recall. There have been a few years in my life when I fasted more days than not. It feels odd saying so as it is not really something that I advertise. However, I do genuinely aspire to live the way that I believe, to the best of my ability.

I was married to a highly abusive and adulterous wife and divorced her – which, by the way, gets a person treated sinfully bad when they're a minister. It really could be summed up to religious abuse from certain church folks during the time when I was having some kind of a breakdown. I was a very legalistic preacher prior to that. While I've always been outrageously kind towards others, I didn't wear shorts, go to the movie theater, and such things that have been traditionally regarded as holiness by old school legalistic Pentecostalism from 14-24 years old. My ex-wife and I vowed before The LORD to go on a 365-day, half-day fast – from midnight till 2PM. Things got worse. We divorced, but my vow unto The LORD still stood. Needless to say, she broke that vow, and I didn't. For the entire year – even while broken and alone – I fasted, grieving deeply and thanking GOD for not abandoning me like so many others had. When I was alone with Him, I still had the precious gift of writing songs. Overall, I've only ever written Gospel songs – I've particularly consecrated that gift to The LORD.

Fast forwarding and jumping over a few things, being the Holy Ghost-filled preacher that I am with an

extensive host of medically verifiable miracles through prayer, as well, and an unwavering faithfulness for GOD – my entry into deliverance ministry was enacting deliverance on myself. The three gatekeeping things that I rebuked, renounced, and cast out were the spirit of rejection, the spirit of heaviness, and subsequently, the root of bitterness. The vast majority of deliverance ministers talk about those things, particularly the two very real demonic offices that I mentioned. They are real, but then so is a spirit of robbery, a spirit of murder, a spirit of hate, a spirit of aloneness, an orphan spirit, and a spirit of nothingness.

While, to the uneducated in these things, I imagine that could sound hokey and made up, I assure you it is not. Often, people in deliverance talk about Jezebel, Leviathan, Satan, Lucifer, and such spirits. Those aren't just names but sorts of offices of the demonic, which ties them to certain objectives and traits. Like the monkey's paw, sin and the demonic always take more than they give. There is always pleasure in it for a season and then ruin, shame, and such. Spirits like Mammon are talked about less commonly. That is a demonic spirit who allows people to attain wealth at an exceedingly high cost – but then this book isn't a non-fiction book explaining all of these things in exquisite detail.

I would say that there are some deliverance ministries who are vastly more competent and adept than others. Certainly, there are some who are not only false but also glorified witchcraft, disguised as Christianity. The issue with that is that witchcraft can't cast out demons – it can only transfer/swap them – which is what you'd read about in studying old Mesopotamian exorcistic rituals for historical academic value, if you were someone like me.

The truth is that the spiritual world is all around us. The reason that witches and pagan cultures believe in the existence of things of a supernatural nature is because they do exist. From a Christian theological standpoint, those religious beliefs all have vestiges of the truth within them, which came in dreams. Jesus Christ is the real thing, the way, the truth, the life, the only way to Heaven. To know Jesus is to know GOD the Father, who sent Him. He is the Son of Man written of in Daniel chapter 7, as was validated by His fulfillment of hundreds of Old Testament prophecies, as well as the copious numbers of miracles that He did while here on earth and is still doing today. As a Christian, I am grafted into the vine – which means Abraham: the father of all who believed.

Since physically being touched by a demon spirit over a year ago and stepping into ministry myself, I've read an extensive amount of books on the subject. I graduated from Dr. Bob Larson's International School of Exorcism, which goes into depth about the history and application of exorcism remarkably well. Amidst my reading, one of the most captivating real-life stories – that I might add is exceedingly too short – is a little book entitled *The Serpent & the Savior: A True Story of Occult-level Spiritual Warfare*, by David El-Cana Bryan. It details how the pastor who wrote that book along with his wife rescued the biological daughter of "The Black Pope" Anton LeVay and then supernaturally killed him – yes, literally killed Anton LeVay – while the diabolical man was attacking the poor woman through astral projection. While this novel that you are about to read would likely have serious potential as a movie, miniseries, or series – I would also personally place that book in the category of one that I'd like to see through the medium of film.

This novel, *Holy Ghost Exorcist*, is based on real-life individuals, real exorcisms, and real events. Some of the life experiences that the fictitious protagonist – Pastor Jackie Noble – are from the real lives of people within ministry who I personally know. Other stories are pulled from the pages of more renowned ministers and authors – who've publicly written and spoken about these experiences – they include Dr. Derick Prince, Dr. Bob Larson, and Apostle Jane Hamon. To the contrary, while I could easily name a list of preachers that you the reader have likely never heard of – I feel like it is better to let them be anonymous. Moreover, I'm only doing that to protect them. It bears noting that all of the big name people that I have mentioned have already drawn a lot of fire for their involvement in deliverance. The quantity and frequency of their attacks is largely because they're bigger targets.

It's my assessment that most people who write screenplays – or perhaps the studios who destroy integrity of well-written screenplays involving exorcistic material – do not know that much about it. Generally, the foe is a super inflated demon – not that there aren't principalities, powers, and the rulers of darkness – which is a completely different thing from an unclean spirit. One is ascribed to fallen angels; the other to the Nephilim. Some wicked spirits are simply stronger than others. It's like the difference between a bobcat and a lion – or perhaps a cruel child and a warring army; both of whom are armed. At any rate, any response worth giving would send me off into preaching to put on the full armor of GOD, and such things. This book is filled with quite a lot of that as it is applicable to the story, and the main character is a preacher who interacts with other preachers.

I would likewise add that in real Christian exorcisms, the name of Jesus is invoked a lot – and not cut from it like Hollywood ignorantly sees fit to do with *The*

Conjuring series and such. While I'm neither endorsing nor denying the integrity of all that Ed & Lorraine Warren did – I only mean to state that if you listen to the recorded audio tapes, there was no shortage of quoting scripture and calling on the name of The LORD Jesus Christ. I would add, that while it is not good to communicate with demons during an exorcistic process any more than necessary – there is a power in calling them out by name, but then that, too, could be said of repentance. A lot of times people want to make things sound cleaner than they are. When what they should do is call things out for exactly what they are – using words/names/acts such as pornography, adultery, masturbation, or whatever might be applicable even if – and especially if – it feels shameful to say. When you hide your sin, it lives another day. That is specifically what sin does to hide. It draws you to do something to feel momentary pleasure and then makes you too ashamed to actively do anything about it, to tell your wife, to tell an accountability partner, or to tell your pastor.

True confession is more like, "Hi, my name is *** and I am an alcoholic." It's not vaguely glossing over your life and saying how that sometimes you don't make the best choices or some other generality. True confession, true confrontation, and true deliverance is always specific. It requires you calling it out by name. Whitewashing sin is folly. Praying in a way that asks GOD to excuse you – as though you couldn't help it – instead of recognizing your wrong and asking for forgiveness has likely sent thousands upon thousands to Hell.

I would also add – both for those in ministry who are getting into deliverance and writers who are looking at this book as the most accurate fictional telling of what life is like for a deliverance minister – that it is good to ask questions, even and by means of paperwork so you know what you're looking for. It is also good to have people there to assist you, lest it is needful. Likewise, you don't want anything in the room that could be weaponized – such as glass – for worst-case scenarios. Questions asked during the preliminary stages of an exorcism would seek to get to the root or often multiple roots of a thing. Where your family descends from, whether any of them have been in the occult or a member of secret societies, whether you or a family member has suffered some kind of trauma, whether there is a habitual sin in your life – such as pornographic addiction, drugs, etc. – whether you harbor unforgiveness towards anyone. Basically, it is an assessment of anything that might open a door giving a legal right to the demonic.

The most complex cases of exorcism are when the person has created multiple personalities to cope with bad things. In such situations, a demon can attach itself to a part of that person and be buried deeper within them. That is difficult to deal with, and someone who is performing an exorcism on a person in that state, or many other fragile states, needs to be careful and have some sort of understanding of psychology so as not to damage them further and create a worse situation than there was at the beginning. No one needs to do anything outside of their capacity to do, spiritually, psychologically, and such. There is a high cost for going in deeper than one ought to. Tragically, there are less competent people who've sought to do exorcisms that have done just that. Dr. Bob Larson is well versed in the exorcism of Emily Rose and the gross negligence that went on during it, leading to the girl's death. He's been where it took place, conversed with the family, and talked about it up to some point in an interview that I was privileged enough to hear. Things like that are terrible. There are appropriate and proper ways of dealing with

them. GOD knows that I could probably write a whole line of books, both fiction and non-fiction regarding my extensive knowledge of the demonic.

It was my presumption that the book *The Serpent and the Savior* only briefly mentioned how Anton LeVay had subjected his daughter to six of the seven rituals of defilement – without naming them – presumably to protect her person. Yet, a part of me feels like people reading should know exactly how vile those practices are. Sewing a human infant up inside of a cow, practicing extreme child sexual abuse, making the person eat excrement, and such things are very real examples of what ceremonial magick and dark arts occultism with the training wheels off look like. I've known of true stories where a young child would be horrifically raped by a man dressed like how they'd imagine the devil to look. Then when the Child called on Jesus to save them, another man within the occult would come into the room dressed like Jesus and rape them. All of this, as well as many other sinister things, were done to break the will of the individual and leave them without hope.

Again, all of these things are matters that I tend to know far more about than most ministers, both on the Christian and Pagan side of things. I understand that witches often have two knives, how one is set aside for gestures, like a wand, and how the other is used as a knife, but both are only set aside for ritual. They also have certain clothes that are set aside for ceremonial use. I understand the difference between a protective circle and triangle when summoning a demonic spirit, why plates with the names of angels written on them are broken as a hoped-for means to emblematically prevent divine intervention regarding the abhorrent things about to take place, the letting of blood and offering of

seminal discharge to the unholy, purification rituals, reverse baptisms, and so forth. Of course most of my knowledge comes from reading books written by occultist for occultists and listening to their teachings intended for like-minded persons – which I'd not recommend for just anyone to do. Less dubious seeming things are not as familiar to me, though I know of them on a more introductory level. I feel that it bears mention that when looking up how to exorcize a demon online – they advise you to burn sage. Rather notably, that is a practice within poison path herbalism, and other forms of witchery. Specifically burning sage is supposed to atmospherically usher in demonic spirits that a Christian or anyone truly wanting to be free from the demonic wouldn't want to summon. Worship ushers in the presence of the Holy Spirit. To put it simply, burning sage is a part of witchcraft and bad information.

In Christendom, full gospel churches have anointing oil, which is usually prayed-over extra virgin olive oil. In the Old Testament, there is a specific formula that GOD called for to make anointing oil, involving certain proportions of cinnamon, cassia, myrrh, etc. Likewise, in witchcraft, they use anointing oil. While there may be variations, the one that I read explained how to make it with mint. There are a lot of things that mean things that most people just don't understand. In Christendom, anointing oil is emblematic to the Holy Spirit. In Catholicism, Holy Water is emblematic to the blood of Christ. Both of these have notably been used in real exorcisms and caused strong visceral reactions from demon spirits that inhabited a person in a way that is advantageous. Likewise, communion has been done in real exorcisms – provoking a reaction from the demonic, as has iconography – specifically a cross throughout Christian exorcisms, and also the priestly stole within Catholicism and Orthodox denominations.

Within Catholicism there are more liturgical prayers. Specifically, the Latin book *Ritvale Romanvm* goes into depth with all of that. There have been a lot of very real, very sincere, devout Catholics who had a genuine relationship with Christ and a great love for people who've practiced extensively as exorcists. It seems sad to me that movies, comic books, and other forms of media after another inappropriately portray so many of them as wayward and carnal, with evident vices such as drinking whiskey, chain smoking, and partaking in other self-indulgent behaviors in excess – rather than pursuing a life filled with holiness as many have done. I would add to all of this that I did enjoy the 2012 horror movie *The Possession*, which had a Jewish exorcist and dealt with the matter of a dybbuk box [*dybbuk* is the Hebrew word for demon as well as a classification of spirit that Dr. Bob Larson says he has confronted]. I also enjoyed the 2023 film *Nefarious*. While the demon never got cast out of the man, I felt like it was conveyed well. The acting was superb, and it was interesting to note that while filming there were heavy supernatural occurrences involving strong winds manifesting out of nowhere to disrupt it and so forth. A real priest was literally on set combating all of that. I mean, honestly, could the film have a better endorsement than that? It goes way deeper because they checked with the weather people and everything to see whether there was anything natural about anything that happened. That's great stuff there.

Certainly, the supernatural, angelic, demonic, exorcisms, faith, and so forth are topics that not only have people found interesting throughout all charted time, but that likewise create an interesting subject matter within fiction as well. I take it all quite seriously, and regardless of what vantage point anyone reading this book comes from, they should appreciate that as my writing might otherwise come off as half done and insincere. With that said, I could rightfully be considered pretty hardcore. I gradually stopped eating pork years ago, I make some strides to try and keep holy days that are ordained by GOD in scripture, and on this past first day of Tishri – on the Hebraic calendar – I began a two-year Nazarite vow because I personally feel compelled too. To be clear, a Nazarite vow is something that most professed Christians don't even know about. In my own personal experience, the majority of church-people who see extreme devotion like my taking a Nazarite vow get offended – or are put off by it rather than rightfully seeing it as faithfulness to GOD. Likewise, those same people get offended when you don't eat or drink something out of some kind of sincere devotion for GOD that they feel is okay to – because they want to beat their chest and scream back that they're just as holy as you.

Let me tell you something. I believe that extreme results come from extreme sacrifice. I know foreigners within ministry who I feel put me to shame. They tell me how great of a man of GOD I am, and when I look at their life, it humbles me and makes me want to cry. Seeing how devout they are makes me feel like a jerk. These wake up and go to bed in the service of The LORD. All they do is teach the Bible and care for orphans, and things like that. Against the backdrop of who they are – I look at myself and think how much better I need to do. I don't get upset over it. The way they live their lives touches my heart. They don't have to reprove me. I see something inside of them that preaches more loud and clear than words ever could. I wanted the character Jackie Noble to be a bit that way. While he has some quirks and idiosyncrasies, I wanted to write a protagonist character that I'd genuinely like and is the clear-cut hero of the story they're in.

No matter who you are, I'd hope that you wouldn't be such a fool that you'd want a pastor who was your drinking buddy. Sensibly, you'd want a pastor who was real, who had an intimate relationship with GOD, who had a good and friendly foundational relationship with you, unlike people who only show up to tell you that you're wrong. Ideally, you'd want a pastor who cared enough about you to tell you the truth in an appropriate way, even when it wasn't what you wanted to hear. You'd want them to likewise live a non-hypocritical life, admitting when he was wrong and atoning for it when possible, as we all should. You'd want someone whose prayers would go past the ceiling and into GOD's throne room. Well, let me tell you, when you're upfront and in the thick of ministry, as well as Southern gospel music – you see and hear a lot of things. Those things are not always good. I've seen behind the curtain.

With that said, I know that hurting people hurt people, and I know that while I've tried to live right, I've done some regrettable things in life, usually to cope from an overwhelming sadness and depression brought on from all of the rejection that I've endured. Still, I remember that starry-eyed little church boy and the preachers I'd look up to. I remember what I really believed that this person or that person was – and I've told myself that I need to be that imagined man of GOD for real, cause one day some little boy or little girl in church is going to look at me, and I don't want to let them down like I was let down. Really, I don't know if there was a disappointment quite like it.

At any rate, in this book I've given you two characters – Pastor Jackie and Penny Noble – that it seems any reasonably-minded person might be able to root for in this story. You're welcome and happy reading.

CHAPTER ONE

The 16th Chapter of Mark

The date was Sunday, August 6th, 1972. As the darkness of night gave way to the morning, the world as men knew it seemed to come to life again. With that, those things living in the shadows returned back unto them as the glorious light from the heavens shone forth. The sweet music of bird songs began to fill the air. All of this was in the background, to be seen and heard from out the window, as Penny Noble filled the coffee pot with water and let the flames from their Kenmore gas stove come up around its bottom. While all of this went on, like a busy bee she went to and fro throughout the kitchen, frying bacon, making cathead biscuits from scratch, frying her husband's eggs over medium and hers over hard.

The couple had no children. They'd met in Bible college. Back then – their sweet courtship had blossomed into an ever deeper love. Then, mere months before his graduation, her husband – Jackie, as everyone knew him – proposed and shortly thereafter wed in 1962.

During the early part of their marriage, Rev. Jackie Noble – who now proudly held a bachelor's degree from Atlanta Christian College of West Point, Georgia – served as a youth minister alongside the Rev. Dr. Byron Phillips at New Life Fellowship Church, not too far from the college campus where Penny still attended.

She was a year behind her husband in school. After earning her bachelor's, the two of them stayed in that town for another seven years, where they labored together with the church's youth department, bus ministry, as well as many other facets.

Handing out thought-provoking illustrated gospel tracts by the artist Jack Chick, Gideon Bibles, and other such things, the couple sought to win the lost and dying world – particularly within the shadow of their church – unto the salvation of the LORD Jesus Christ. Once a year, Penny would write a church play in hopes that sinners – who'd otherwise never darken the door of a church for service – might come to watch a theatrical presentation instead. At the end of each heartfelt performance, Dr. Phillips would give an altar call.

GOD gave the Nobles souls for their labors. Yet, their work wasn't limited to this. Jackie would play the guitar and have worship services at one of the local nursing homes. He and Penny would occasionally donate their time at a soup kitchen. Likewise, they'd travel into the city to rally against the unthinkable act of murdering children through abortion clinics. Jackie would preach how it was a travesty upon the land, reciting how its founder Margaret Sanger admittedly began the practice to exterminate the negro race, additionally giving scientifically proven facts in regards to the development of a baby within its mother's womb, as well as quoting passages such as Jeremiah 1:5, which says,

"Before I formed thee in the belly I knew thee, and before thou comest forth out of the womb I sanctified thee, and I ordained thee a prophet unto the nations."

The Nobles had hearts of compassion, practicing what they preached and living what they believed. Their house had no television set as they and their denomination believed that it corrupted the anointing. Neither of them wore wedding bands, as they considered jewelry to be a vain thing – nor did Penny Noble have her ears pierced for both that reasoning and the line of thinking that it'd be marring her flesh – despite any favorable passages that someone might say otherwise about GOD putting a nose ring in His bride and so forth. Jackie had shortly cut, preacherly hair, the top of which was jointly combed to the side and back with some Brylcreem. Penny's hair was long, full, and straight; if worn down, it'd come somewhere within the proximity of her mid-thigh. To state it plainly, they were an extraordinarily clean-looking couple who seemed like everything that old-school church had been. Stylistically, Rev. Jackie Noble would say pithy little things from the pulpit, such as,"I read the Bible and I read the newspaper, so I know both sides of the story." And that really just sums up how he and his quiet and submissive wife felt about it.

Jackie loved Penny so much. He'd die for her. The Nobles had no children because Penny was unable to conceive. How much more horrible was it for her to look on and see some of the same women returning time and time again, using the nearby abortion clinics as a form of birth control? Having a heart filled with love and compassion, she would compel them to turn away from such wickedness – and some would. Howbeit, she still looked on, watching as so many other girls seemed to believe the industrial complex's lies to be a convenient truth, thus allowing them to live a more self-indulgent life perceivably escaping the consequences for the choices they'd made. She wondered about so many of them.

How many of these women were discernibly subject to the blood curse they'd brought upon themselves by murdering their innocent child? How many of them remembered each year how old their dead son or daughter would be had they given them the gift of life? Certainly some would – and had. Her heart of gold wept so heavily for both lives that were being destroyed with each visit to an abortionist – not to mention the doctors, nurses, and everyone else complicit in the dealing of death that went on behind those closed doors.

At the end of the day, Penny could only give GOD thanks for those she'd reached, and so she did. Those who'd turned away from this darkness allowed her to feel like it was worth it all. Some of them had elected to raise their children, while others put their children up for adoption. In either case, it thrilled her heart so. This was who she and her husband were.

While there was a building in town solely devoted to the shedding of innocent blood and snuffing out the lives of unborn babies, Penny Noble and her beloved Jackie were saving them. Moreover in all of this, there was one girl who couldn't turn to her family due to the shame she had brought them. Her name was Annette. The young couple let her live with them through the remainder of her pregnancy as well as during the first year of her baby's life.

They did all that they could to help her get on her feet. During the time of her residence with the couple, she met a young widower named Roger Clark at their church. Annette became more active, the two of them hit it off, and once they wed, Annette and her beautiful baby, David, from then on lived with him. It seemed the perfect situation. The child had a father and mother who loved him. They were part of an active and loving church body. Each day seemed to be an indicator that the Nobles were doing everything right as they pressed forward in the ways of the LORD.

Whereas Penny – like most women at that time – was a housewife, Jackie worked at a store selling shoes. It was a modest living. Howbeit, whereas the two of them did so much at the church and it had grown up to a nice size, they gained a small wage from there as well. Everything that they had was the LORD's and the LORD was their everything.

The coffee pot whistled, thus indicating that the boiling water was primed to come cascading through the mug which held, at the bottom, Rev. Jackie Noble's favorite brand of instant coffee. As Penny poured, he entered the kitchen to sit down by his made plate and have the cup of hot joe handed to him by his sweet wife.

"Good to the last drop," she said.

"What's wrong with the last drop?" he questioned.

The two of them grinned at each other for a moment, probably feeling the whole affair was funnier than it was, and then Penny began telling Jackie about the letter that she'd received the other day. It was from Annette. She, Roger, and David would be coming through town in the next few weeks and hoped that they could all get together during that time. You see, since everything aforementioned Jackie and Penny's life had taken a new direction. Given his success as a youth pastor at one church, he was offered to take a church as his own within their particular Pentecostal denomination in 1970.

Returning to the present: two years within their pastorate had passed and the church had transitioned from a sparsely attended church under the previous pastorate to a medium-sized congregation with room to grow. In fact, as of the previous Sunday, their church had forty people. The numbers did seem to move a bit. Fifty people wouldn't be odd. Sixty people might be there for a semi-special occasion. Their seating capacity would hold 125 in a single service. If they brought in metal folding chairs, they could accommodate as many as 160 people, but it was tight – really tight. And he knew. They once hosted a community service where some of the other area churches came together with them. People were nearly spilling out the door and into the street.

But today, August 6th, 1972, was just a regular Sunday, or so the two of them thought. Howbeit, this was the day when two young men would come and visit their little church and subsequently set off a chain of events that'd turn Jackie and Penny's world upside down. Their names were Henry Farmer and George Bean.

As they arrived at Souls Harbor Holiness Church nearly an hour and a half before service, Pastor Jackie got a broom out of the closet and began to sweep the pollen and such off of the church's front porch and parking lot. There were a few spiderwebs in the railings too that pretty well every week had to be knocked down, or else they'd be thicker the next week. This wasn't supposed to look like a haunted house after all, but a holy house. The only ghost inside their place was The Holy Ghost. Penny went around doing some hit-and-miss dusting. God had been good to them. They and the congregation had recently raised the funds for a baby grand piano. They'd bought it used, had it hauled, had it

tuned, and marveled at how it looked and sounded new.

Within nearly twenty-five minutes of them being there, other helpers arrived. Brother Vincent, and Shirley, and Sister Young came in immediately, cleaning the bathrooms, changing light bulbs, and such. Jack had already begun brewing some coffee for them in the kitchen adjoined to their church fellowship hall – which lay in the basement of their building. Before long, Sunday school would start. One after another, their parishioners trickled in. There were about fifteen adults in Sunday school that day, eleven kids in the children's class, and three young ones in the nursery. Linda Edwards' husband, Tony, taught the class, though it generally turned more into revivalistic preaching than teaching – and he was a hacker.

Whereas the day's lesson was supposed to be on the life of Job, it somehow transmuted into a tale of his and others' experiences of trial and tribulation. Periodically, he'd come back to the subject at hand, only to leave it again. The lesson – if you could call it that – was filled with whoops and hollers; people shouting "Amen," "Glory, Hallelujah," and "I've got the victory!" Linda reminded her husband how Pastor Jackie and Penny had told them of the special guests they'd have visiting next Sunday. Interrupting himself, Brother Tony then stopped midway through the announcement – which again came more off like a fiery sermon – by calling the pastor's wife up to tell everyone a little more about it.

In the most heartfelt way imaginable, Sister Penny Noble walked up to the platform and began to speak about a great evil that had come across the land, known as abortion. She spoke of the countless lives that are slaughtered each and every day. And emphasized the sinful sexual liberation movement that was going on – where women who'd identifiably recognized the wicked foolishness of men's sexual exploits dubiously determined that they were going to be as much or worse fiends than their male counterparts.

"That's why we actively stand against this injustice that further victimizes women under what our audacious government wickedly calls 'women's rights.' The Bible says in the 24th chapter of Proverbs, 'Deliver those who are drawn toward death, and hold back those stumbling to the slaughter. If you say, Surely we did not know this, does not He who weighs the hearts consider it? He who keeps your soul, does He not know it?'"

She talked further, reminding them of a woman, who'd visited to speak the previous year, who had saline burns all over her body from when her mother tried to kill her in her womb. The abortion clinic workers there took her and put her in a closet, under a pillow to die, but a faithful pro-life woman rushed into the clinic, snatched her up in her arms, and raised her as her own. Hers was but one of hundreds – and in time, maybe even one of the thousands of stories like this. Then someone else burst out about a lady they knew who'd had an abortion and lived in unending grief because of what the wicked doctors had done to her. She was young back at the time when it happened, and she believed their lies. Her story was one of redemption. She later came to Jesus Christ, got married, had two children, and will one day be with her other child in Heaven, where she'll see that precious little girl who's never known the heartache of this world.

There was hardly a dry eye in the house as the adults' extended Sunday school class went over due to all of this. More people came in bit by bit during this time. Most seemed to become stirred by the heartfelt emotion and testimonies there in the room. Among them were a few new visitors. Some were families, young and old. Likewise, there were a few individuals, some of whom had a friend with them. They ranged in their appearances. Some were a bit churchy looking, some casual, and others perhaps didn't know a thing about church or the Bible. Those persons looked as though they'd lived hard lives. Still, all were welcome, and Souls Harbor Holiness Church was thankful for each and every one.

After all of this, the Sunday Morning worship service began. Betty Sue Riley quietly arose from her seat and seemingly drifted up to the glorious baby grand piano almost unnoticed amid the whoops, stage-whisper prayers, and lifted exaltations to the King of Glory. From thence, she began to rhythmically crank out some upbeat Pentecostal sounds comprised of rocking five-finger beats, running alongside some two- and three-finger chords that, as far as anyone there was concerned, made those black and ivory keys sing out as though it was coming from the fancy concert hall. In unison, the congregation appeared to rise, with only the new visitors lagging a bit behind but trying to fit in and standing as well. All throughout the auditorium folks went to clapping, lifting their hands in praise, and stirring about. Some did something of a little two-step or twist where they stood to the flow of the music - praising the LORD with their dance. Joining in on all of this was their worship leader Sister Martha, who flowed with the music and sang songs like "That's Him," "Old Time Religion," and "He Set Me Free." Just like waves, the power and presence of the Holy Ghost began to ripple across that sanctuary from front to back, and the whole church could feel it. It was Brother Leroy who first took off running and there went Bobby Joe right after him. Sister Barton started hollering,

"Hallelujah! Hallelujah! Thank you, Jesus!"

Folks were carrying on and worshiping The Lord for what seemed over an hour. It was around about the time when the United Methodist Church down the road was letting out that Souls Harbor Holiness Church's pastor got up to begin his sermon.

"Now friends, we didn't come here today to play patty-cake but to worship the Lord of Hosts. Ain't you glad to be worshiping the King?" said Pastor Jackie, pausing for dramatic emphasis.

"I know that other churches are getting out right about now, but while The Church of Christ down the road might be concerned with being the first ones down at the local buffet, our concern oughta be being the Church that Christ called us to be! From what we've felt – and seen – and heard today, you and I both know that I could not say another word, and we could all rightfully tell everybody that we had church here in this place. But, GOD gave me a word to speak to you and it is my prayer that you'll receive it this morning," said he.

All throughout this and during this timed pause, the livelier congregants hollered out Yeses and Amens with such vigorous enthusiasm that anyone might think that they were otherwise in a contest to see who was the most spiritual.

Pastor Jackie Noble's key text came from Hebrews 10:19-31, which reads as follows:

"Therefore, brethren, having boldness to enter the Holiest by the blood of Jesus, by a new and living way which He consecrated for us, through the veil, that is, His flesh, and having a High Priest over the house of God, let us draw near with a true heart in full assurance of faith, having our hearts sprinkled from an evil conscience and our bodies washed with pure water. Let us hold fast the confession of our hope without wavering, for He who promised is faithful. And let us consider one another in order to stir up love and good works, not forsaking the assembling of ourselves together, as is the manner of some, but exhorting one another, and so much the more as you see the Day approaching. For if we sin willfully after we have received the knowledge of the truth, there no longer remains a sacrifice for sins, but a certain fearful expectation of judgment, and fiery indignation which will devour the adversaries. Anyone who has rejected Moses' law dies without mercy on the testimony of two or three witnesses. Of how much worse punishment, do you suppose, will he be thought worthy who has trampled the Son of God underfoot, counted the blood of the covenant by which he was sanctified a common thing, and insulted the Spirit of grace? For we know Him who said, 'Vengeance is Mine, I will repay,' says the Lord. And again, 'The Lord will judge His people.' It is a fearful thing to fall into the hands of the living God."

As he spoke these words of scripture, they seemed to cut through the air like thunder. Now only a few people belted out an "Amen," "C'mon," or "Preach,"

to add emphasis. And while most pastors might try to accommodate the largely hushed audience by telling them how he knew that this wasn't a shouting message, the sermon instead appropriately began – in following the scripture – with him relating how the Old Testament exemplified the weightiness of sin and the power of The Law. After all, those who transgress any part of the law have transgressed in the whole and are thereby damned to an eternal burning Hell. The high priests had to do temporary things which thereby pointed to the redemptive blood of the one who was both GOD and man – Jesus Christ – which Daniel 7, and so many other passages prophesied. In fact the two powers in Heaven, neither of whom was a created being, both being GOD, were taught among many of the rabbis during the second temple period. From there the sermon carefully illustrated Christ's fulfillment of the Messianic covenant – being an appropriation for the sins of man, grafting the Gentiles into the Abrahamic covenant with Him as though merging wild olive branches with natural Israel from whence salvation came.

It was a reversal of what had taken place at the tower of Babel and a fulfillment of GOD calling all people back to His goodness: to any who would come. Moreover, it was a strict call to Holiness – to make our bodies a living sacrifice, holy and acceptable before GOD, which is our reasonable service. The good news of the gospel was presented alongside the ever-present reality of an eternal burning Hell. With immense competence, Pastor Noble even sighted how there were many Jewish texts that also pounded these points outside of the Biblical canon, which was, as they saw it, the King James translation Bible. As he preached, some began to tremble as they were filled with the conviction of the Holy Spirit, having heard these words.

Before his sermon came to a close, someone cried out boisterously, "Oh, dear GOD – I repent! Save me! I am a wretched sinner!" as they came running to an altar as if their life was in immediate jeopardy. With that, a wailing from a second and profuse sobbing from a third sounded out through the church house. Being of the old school, rather than bringing his message to an abrupt close, Pastor Jackie continued onward, allowing those crying out to GOD to actually communicate with Him uninterrupted. Some knelt down with those at the altar, praying softly. Others stretched their hands forward – as it was in the direction of those people – and to the first person's side was a congregant egging them on, saying things like, "Just call upon the LORD and He will hear you," and "GOD is gracious to forgive." Likewise, as he came to a finish, Pastor Jackie gave a formal altar call, as it was not GOD's will that any perish. After bidding the lost to come, he asked those who wished to have a closer walk with Christ to find an altar and pray. For all others, he asked that they'd pray with those who were praying.

Like a good and faithful shepherd, he was there for the sheep of this fold, thoughtfully praying for each of them. Penny did likewise, as did some of the elders of their church. Then finally, after all of this, he asked if anyone had a need of prayer for their body, a financial need, and so forth. To this, one couple asked that they be prayed for as they were trying to conceive a baby. The pastor took a prayer cloth, explained how the Apostle Paul had done likewise with handkerchiefs and such, anointed it with oil, and gave it to the couple to put under a pillow in their marriage bed. After this, someone else came up who said that they had a lot of pain in their lower back. The pastor gently placed his hand over the aching area and commanded any ailment to leave in the authoritative name of Jesus Christ, and it was so. Jumping up and down, the man whose back pain was healed began to run around the church shouting praises of thanksgiving unto the LORD. And thus, their altar service continued with people trembling under the power of the Holy Ghost, being slain in The Spirit, speaking in, praying in, and singing in tongues under a thick revivalistic anointing.

With all hearts and minds clear, as it has long been church etiquette to say before a benedictory prayer, it was 3:30 in the afternoon before their morning service let out, and thereby only two and a half hours until they'd reconvene for the evening service. Pastor Jackie and Penny stood near the door as folks were leaving the service. They and others hugged and shook hands with their fellow congregants. Church members conversed with greeters. Moreover, the pastor was allowed time to catch everyone before they left. Many would be back that evening – yet due to the work schedules of some – all would not. Out of all of the people that he spoke to, the last two to approach Pastor Jackie were the afore-named Henry Farmer and George Bean.

Henry was tall and thin with coarse brown hair and a few freckles dotting his face around his nose. He wore a dark-colored suit that looked slightly wrinkled with pants that were almost too short, barely exposing the tan socks inside his patent leather wing-tipped shoes. His cohort, George, was a long, shaggy, dishwater-blonde-haired teenager with bright blue eyes and sun-kissed skin. The boy was either trying to grow a beard or had a desperate need for a razor, if not both. The scraggly mess nonetheless made him distinctive. While Henry seemed to want to look more like he was from Chicago or someplace, via his fancy duds, George looked like more of a surfer type, wearing a Hawaiian shirt with khaki pants and a black leather belt and donning a pair of penny loafers.

Jackie smiled invitingly and extended his hand to both of these young men. "God bless you," he said, then added, "Welcome to Souls Harbor Holiness Church." Smiling back at him, the two of them only spoke with Jackie Noble briefly, telling him how much they enjoyed it. The remainder of their conversation revolved around the boys' shoes, as Jackie was a man in the shoe business and knowledgeable on all things shoes. And while neither of them would return for service that Sunday night, he had made quite an impression on these two young men and unbeknownst to him he was about to find out how much in the strangest of ways in the not-so-distant future.

The evening service was a time filled with just as much fire, celebration, prayer, praise, and individual testimonies as one might expect to ride on the back of that morning's blowout. Additionally, they would "have church," as it is phrased, during their Wednesday night service as well. Outside of the ministerial realm of things, though, Jackie Noble's life was a quiet one. He'd wake up each morning reading several chapters of the Bible. Pray when waking, going to bed, before meals, and take time both to intercede and commune with the Father throughout the day. In his 1967 Chevrolet Station Wagon, he had an 8-track player. At that particular time, it had The Hemphill's album, *Old Brush Arbor Days*, by Canaan Records (circa 1970). Whereas it was an 8-Track, the tracks as listed on the LP would have 3 consecutive songs on each of the 4 tracks. The LP's track list was as follows:

TRACK #1

A1	Old Brush Arbor Days	2:25
A2	An Unfinished Task	4:15
A3	Shoutin' On the Hills	1:59

TRACK #2

A4	God's Gonna Shake This World Again	4:13
A5	Jesus Is Coming Soon	2:01
A6	You're a Living Soul	2:51

TRACK #3

B1	Sing Me a Happy Song	2:00
B2	Through Faith I Still Believe	3:25
B3	Hallelujah, Anyhow	2:07

TRACK #4

B4	Move Up a Little Closer	1:49
B5	No Disappointment in Jesus	2:02
B6	On the Way Up	2:51

Jackie would listen to it, basking in the warmth of GOD's love to the sweet sounds of Southern gospel music. Every now and then, he'd get so stirred up that tears of joy would fill his eyes as he thought about the goodness of GOD. More than not, these private praise sessions were on his way to and from work – where he reaped a commission from selling shoes at the J.C. Penny department store and he loved his job. Jackie was a shoe salesman that people could trust. He got them what they wanted in the right fit and built a relationship with his customers the way that a doctor or someone in any other line of work might. There was a personality to it and – as one might think – being a preacher, it was ideal that he'd be a pretty personable guy.

Jackie knew his frequent customers by name. While many of them didn't know him as a pastor, he was a warm light of encouragement and hope in their lives that they could trust. Due to his long-term involvement with selling shoes, shoes sometimes became a metaphor utilized in his sermons. To him, it seemed to work well. After all, it was far less racy than other subjects.

Besides that, the fact that he worked at the J.C. Penny department store and had a wife named Penny was not lost on him. Jackie would tell far too many people things like, "I work for Penny's," then add, "Penny's clothes," and "Penny's food," and from there, the list went on and on into what he thought of as pure comedy. It'd be that next Thursday at work when he'd next see that young man, Henry Farmer, who'd visited the church days before.

"Hey-ya, Preach," a friendly voice exclaimed. Drawing his eyes towards the call, there was Henry; howbeit, this time he wasn't wearing the prestigious patent leather shoes as before but rather a pair of beat-up, falling apart sneakers.

"Oh, Henry…it's good to see you again, son. Don't know if I can say the same for those shoes, though," the reverend told him.

"Yessir. They've sure seen better days. Somebody told me down at the church where you pastor that you worked here. They were complimenting my dress shoes. Really, those are the only good pair that I've got. These are my more casual ones, but as you can see, they're about to head out the door," Henry answered.

"I sure can," Jackie replied in a jolly, humorous kind of way, with a slight twinkle in his eye. And thus his joint role of shoe salesman and minister flawlessly went underway.

Jackie had a fine balancing act that he could maintain of talking to people about shoes and telling them about the LORD Jesus Christ, practically all in the same breath. He was just that kind of guy. The sneakers that Henry wore were falling apart. The toe of them was coming unstitched and ever so slightly opened like a mouth as he walked. Nice as they had once been, those shoes didn't have long. Jackie had owned a pair like that when he was a boy. He told Henry about it. He used to wear them to play baseball. It was a game that his young heart came to love and still did.

His favorite team had been, was, and would always be the Atlanta Braves. He could still remember as a boy when they won the World Series in 1957, how they also won the National League Pennant that same year – and won it again the year after that. Sure, there were lots of other great teams out there, but Georgia had and would always be home to Jackie and the Atlanta Braves would thereby always be his favorite baseball team.

Within the next twenty minutes or so, Pastor Jackie and Henry had gotten to know each other quite a bit more, and whereas they both loved Georgia, Jesus, and baseball, one might say it was a smooth beginning. In fact the two of them even talked to each other about where they lived, though how that came about seemed obvious enough…Jackie had asked Henry, "So, do you live far from the church?" and it all went from there. By the time they were done talking, Henry knew the exact house where Pastor Noble lived, as Pastor Noble knew Henry's. It was even suggested that perhaps the preacher might come over to the young Mr. Farmer's home and watch a Braves game with his family and a few of their friends, as it was some sort of a social get-together that happened there.

"I just might take you up on that," Jackie answered him with a smile.

And thus was their second encounter at J.C. Penny's department store on a Thursday.

When he returned home from work, Jackie told his wife, Penny – not to be confused with the store – that she'd never guess who he ran into today. Being a woman with what seemed to be a clear sense of discernment, she answered correctly. Smiling and carrying on a bit over it, Penny then explained how Henry had a brief conversation with her where he modestly told how the dress shoes he was wearing were the only good ones that he had. She took it as a sign from the LORD; after all, how could he know that her husband was a shoe salesman? One thing led to another, and there the two of them met again.

As Jackie and Penny turned in for the night, they discussed how excited they were that Annette, her little David, and Roger would be in town Saturday and again on Sunday, when they'd asked her to get up and share her testimony. All went as expected. Their reunion was warm and welcoming. Annette got up and brought many people to tears as she told about how young and impressionable she was as a girl, being coerced to murder her baby in her womb by a crooked culture that no longer seemed to blush at their sin. Her son Davie, of course, added to the presentation as she talked about new life, GOD's redemption, and how He will make a way when there seems to be no way.

Annette thanked the Nobles for how they'd helped her, given her a roof to live under, and how it was them taking her to New Life Fellowship Church, where she met her dear husband, Roger. Those meeting her for the first time within Souls Harbor Holiness Church felt like family. They'd tell her things about how their Spirit – or rather the Spirit of the LORD within them – bore witness with hers. While geographically divided by some miles, they were all one within the body of Christ.

The couple left the Nobles' home midday that same Sunday. On Monday morning, Jackie got up for work and everything was as it usually was. Likewise, such was the case on Tuesday, Wednesday, and Thursday. Like a clock ticking down – of which he was unaware – that Friday was the day when everything would start to change.

It was a Friday afternoon – the date of August 18th, 1972 – when a knock came at the Nobles' door. Moments before the frantic knocking, a car had sped along the road, running off of the street across the sidewalk and into the front lawn of the family's yard. Rushing from the vehicle, which was still left running was Henry Farmer, who was joined by his cohort George Bean. With something boarding a kind of hysteria, the two of them began to knock on the pastor's front door in tandem. Answering the door, Penny called out to her husband that he had some visitors – and whereas he was a pastor, this could mean anything.

Rather than coming inside, as no real amount of time had elapsed during their waiting to talk with him, the two of them both looked ecstatic in a gleeful way as well as shocked in a jarring sense.

"Hello, boys. What brings the two of you by this evening?" Pastor Jackie asked.

From there on out, the two of them began to relay to him the life-altering decision they had both made to follow Jesus Christ. They continued to tell the reverend how genuine they both felt that he was, and began to recount the verses that close out the book of Mark: most specifically, Christ's first commission gave of them as an evident sign of any true follower of His, which involved having the power and authority to cast out demons in Jesus' name. And while that is easy to say in church speak, the common practice of it seemed to dissipate severely after Constantine institutionalized the church. Before those times, everything that The Church did was in power and authority and at the cost of their lives. Christianity thrived under persecution and was at its strongest when it was come up against.

Howbeit, when the church became a state religion, it became profitable to have an office within its walls. It helped one's notoriety to be within its fellowship. All earthly consequences seemed to cease and the rewards seemed endless. Thus insincere persons joined its ranks, many historically paid to rise in power. Those whom GOD would deem unworthy to preach the gospel instead preached lies in an effort to build their own kingdoms rather than the kingdom of GOD. Still, everything that these two boys were saying was entirely true. The real church, GOD's church – those who are really saved, sanctified, and filled with the Holy Ghost – certainly should have the power to cast out demons in Jesus' name. And thereafter came what they were building to.

It was George who first blurted out that there was a man possessed by the devil, and then Henry began saying something about it. Quite frankly, the two of them began to talk over each other in such a way that what they were saying both made some kind of jumbled-up sense, though it was also indiscernible all at the same time. At any rate, one thing led to another, and Pastor Jackie Noble found himself going along with the two of them to see what this whole situation was really about.

Rather than riding in their car, the reverend elected to take them in his, thus prompting Henry to turn his car off and call out, "Shotgun!" So off they went. As they traveled, the two of them began to tell the grim details of how others had told them of this demonized individual who lived in isolation, unwashed, unkept, and unholy. The person in question had been into drugs, pornography, horror movies, and rock music. Some way, somehow, unbeknownst to them, this young man had opened some kind of door between the physical and metaphysical – which, as they saw it, had allowed for something to come in.

For two teenagers so new to the faith, their abundance of perception was remarkable, considering that is what was going on rather than a series of bad trips. Jackie knew all about that; he'd slipped and tried a few things during his formative years, and he'd seen other things. He knew how sin veiled itself just enough so you couldn't make out whether this thing before you was a friend or a foe. Thus an intelligent evil would entice its prey until the person eventually found themselves helpless in its web. If they should separate themselves from this familiar evil, it'd work its sympathetic magic, such as reminding the woman of when the man bought her flowers, all while neglecting to mention how he cursed and beat her five minutes afterward. With such

efforts the demonic has lured so many people back into its grasp. The poor fools know not that it is for their lives, nor that Hell widens its mouth awaiting the hour it might swallow them whole.

As the three of them came closer and closer to the location of the presumed demoniac, they journeyed that much further off of the beaten path. Somewhere, where maps will not take you, is where he was found – back in the woods, in that place lined only with gravelless, dirty paths used as roads and bullet-ridden "No Trespassing" signs – sat a rusty and dilapidated black and yellow school bus, once belonging to GOD only knows what school district from GOD only knows when. And yet, as remote of a place as this was, as though from out of the woods or somewhere unbeknownst to the Reverend Jackie Noble, came an amassment of teenagers, folks in their early to mid-twenties, and even a small handful of children with them as if some sort of entertainment was about to take place before their eyes. One woman, who had uncombed hair that seemed likely to have something crawling in it, had at least half of one of her sweat-sheened breasts exposed from out of her three-quarters unbuttoned blouse so as to nurse her baby amidst the other men, women, and children gathered all around her. They certainly were an unkempt lot of people at that, the likes of which few have seen and lived to tell about it.

Still, having arrived, now with even more tension in the air than otherwise expected, Jackie stepped out of his station wagon.

"He's on the bus," said George, and then he began to point at this ghastly abomination that once might have been a relatively normal school bus. Moss, rust, and mud adorned it.

The excrement of ten thousand birds had been drizzled over it. This bus' cracks and dents were the resting places and home to the stagnant waters where a million mosquitoes were born and frogs came to relieve themselves. And despite all of this, the man of GOD was now there and this was the habitation where all eyes looked for him to enter. And thus he wondered, is this where evil resides?

The stained and crusted-over windows on the inside allowed just enough light to make out the shapes of shadows and colors of objects whether living or stationary. Up toward the front, in what would be considered the second row of seats by any school bus driver, reclined a young person who was indistinguishable as either a male or female due to their exceedingly thin frame and long, unwashed hair. A needle was sticking out of their arm, and thus Jackie spoke kindly to them both as a statement and a question.

"I'm told that there is a demon here," he said.

"A demon? Yeah, man. We all have our demons. Guess you're talking about Larry, though. Larry's got a devil," rang out the oscillating helium-sounding voice of the stoner youth, who then staggered around the pastor as though to get off of the bus, but instead flopped backward into the bus driver's seat with their back against the large old steering wheel.

"Larry's got a demon. Larry's got a demon," the voice continuously chanted in a "nah-nah-nah-nah-nah" mocking, rhythmic tone.

And thus with that arose a figure from the seat before the last. Somewhat veiled in shadow, and the smoke of whatever these kids had been smoking in that bus, stood a man whose age was difficult to guess. His body was emaciated and covered with sores, bruises, scrapes, and cuts. His hair hung down in a long, stringy array – though not the way it'd look naturally. It looked more like it had been long and chunks had systematically been cut or torn out by the roots, thus attributing to some random bald patches on his head. The area as to where a gentleman's beard might grow was the same. Most similarly, he looked like a dog with the mange. Also, when he opened his mouth, his oral hygiene, or lack thereof not only followed this horrific theme but added to it. From the looks and smell of it, Jackie wondered whether his mouth was full of rot, blood, excrement, or any combination of those, not precluding that he might have missed an item or two in his assessment.

All during this juggling act of the Reverend Jackie Noble, pastor of Souls Harbor Holiness Church, taking in the surreal horror and complete oddness of this whole affair, the heavily salivating man before him began to go into a state of angry looking, tremorous joltings while taking small, ridged steps away from where he'd been lying and towards the intruding Man of GOD. In some sort of incoherent mutterings ejaculating from out of the person seemed to emit what sounded like some sort of uncommon tribal tongue – and then came English.

"Who do you think that you are to come to this place at this time?" the demon speaking and puppeteering the tragic young man, known only to Pastor Noble as Larry, asked through him.

Howbeit, it was a rhetorical question, for not more than a second and a half later, the thing cried out in the harshest of tones the word, "DIE." Between telling the pastor to die several more times, it let out an inhuman, agonizing dual-toned shrieking howl that sounded like a bass singer gargling mixed with a lion's growl on the lower octave. While on the higher end, he projected a vocal emission somewhere among the auditory effects of nails on a chalkboard, styrofoam being rubbed together, and what one might imagine a pterosaur to sound like. As all of this happened, the man's body began to metamorphose to some degree, becoming more animalistic in the way it moved in such a way that he lept atop one of the bus seats in a feral, almost perching manner and pounced across the aisle, frontward, again and again, in rapid succession, without ceasing for a moment, to cry aloud for the minister's utter demise. All the while, the constant singing of, "Larry's got a demon!" continued on unhindered until finally, Jackie Noble cried out,

> "In the name of the Lord Jesus Christ, come out!" Then everything changed. As if thrown into the wall of the school bus, the unkempt man leapt over Larry, defying gravity and physics, and began swirling from his normal course of movement into a barrel roll that sent him crashing, sliding, and being pressed into the wall. Jackie swore that he felt the bus move from the impact but kept on.

> "I said, in the name of Jesus Christ, come out!" the preacher again cried.

The congregation of people outside of the bus could hear everything, only imagining the spectacle that was taking place inside the derelict vehicle. Then, moments later, the druggy from the front seat began proclaiming how that preacher cast the devil out of Larry by the power of the LORD Jesus Christ in a sort of verbiage filled with heavy expletives as one would never hear during a testimony in church. Meanwhile, Larry had thrown up several times; then, thereafter, he and the preacher were talking. The poor young man accepted Jesus into his heart there on that day.

As life would have it, someone was there with a McDonald's hamburger, fries, and a Mountain Dew for Larry's consumption.

"I told you he could do it," said Henry.

"Yeah, well I told 'em too," argued George.

"Boys, it was the LORD who did it. Just like the fire inside the burning bush didn't make the bush great, but was instead great inside that bush – so is His Spirit inside of me," Jackie told them.

With tear-filled eyes he began to talk to all of these strange people who were there about how the souls of mankind have been in great peril since the beginning, for an evil army seeks to destroy us and drag every person to Hell, but amidst this very real and dreadful fear, GOD's message is a message of hope, which tells how He loved us all so much while we were yet sinners that Jesus came down and took our place. If you received Jesus into your hearts, tell Him that you're sorry for following all of those things that leave you empty, and dedicate your life to Him – then you can have this freedom that he offers, living together with a GOD who loves you.

There he stayed, listened to, talked with, and prayed over these poor, wayward people up into the night. Thankfully, another miracle from GOD happened when he made it back home. Henry, George, and Jackie could do little more than praise the Lord of the Hosts of Heaven while Henry periodically gave him directions to turn here or there. For a while, Jackie even cranked up his car stereo to the sound of The Hemphill's so these boys could hear what real music sounded like. When he got home he told his wife everything.

Yes, that was the night that EVERYTHING changed.

CHAPTER 02

The Exorcism of Betty Sue Riley

Very early Saturday morning – August 19th, 1972 – hours after the school-bus exorcism, Jackie Noble was wide awake, boiling water for a cup of his favorite instant coffee and scrambling around like a madman who lacked some idea of how to do things in regards to making the two of them breakfast. Nonetheless, Penny was delighted to see him trying.

"What's this that I see? Was my man gonna make me breakfast in bed?" Penny asked with a delightful chuckle buried somewhere beneath the question.

"Something like that," he responded with a one-sided grin and half wink thrown in her direction.

"Here, here, you're making a mess."

"Whoops! Let me help you with that."

"Be careful, dear."

– and "I love you" were all phrases that rolled off of the tongue of Penny Noble. She was so proud of the Man of GOD that she had married and so grateful for the miraculous deliverance that had happened last night within the deep dark woods of Georgia – parts unknown.

As Jackie sipped his coffee, he let out an audible "mmm," likely indicating that Maxwell House's instant coffee was so delightful that even he could make it right.

"The coffee is good?" Penny said in an inquisitively playful manner, as if it were a question that really needed asking.

"All the time," Jackie retorted in something of a choral church jest.

Therein, playing along it seemed that the only thing for Penny to do was to echo back, "All the time…"
To which Jackie responded, "The coffee is good."
[A church joke that the unconverted just wouldn't understand.]

Then turning to seriousness, Penny addressed how he was up all night. She told him that she'd heard him praying and praising, and how she knew that the events of the day really touched him. Moreover, she told him that she knew that the LORD had touched a lot of people and expressed how humbling it was that, of all people GOD had used their household to do it through.

It was sometime during their breakfast – and Jackie's third cup of coffee – that a knock came at the door. It was a gentleman from the local newspaper who was hearing all kinds of talk about what had happened. He added how he'd been hearing some stories about it. The boy from whom Jackie had exorcized the demon had been tied up in really bad things for such a long time. His family thought he'd gone completely crazy. Allegedly, that boy named Larry came home and went to tearing down band posters off of his bedroom wall, smashing rock albums to pieces, dumping drug paraphernalia over here, flushing and burning things over there.

"Sounds kind of like Elisha," Jackie said.

"Someone you know?" the reporter asked.

"He's from the Bible: the Prophet Elisha. He slaughtered his cattle and burned every bridge so he would have nothing to turn back to and no place to go but after GOD," Jackie answered.

"If you say so, Rev.," the reporter replied.

The two of them talked for a good little while before Pastor Jackie told the man that he was gonna have to get going pretty soon. When the reporter told him that he understood a man like himself must live a pretty busy life, Jackie volunteered that he was going down, accompanied by Penny – per their discussion last night – to the creek to baptize some of those young people who'd accepted Jesus Christ that evening. With the Reverend's permission, the newsman followed him, snapped a few photographs, and asked the far smaller grouping that was surrounding the school bus exorcism about all that had occurred. And while he talked to this one and that one, the one that he most wanted to talk to was Larry.

Still looking rough from years of using, Larry now had a clean-shaven head and face. He was wearing a clean, tucked-in t-shirt, pants, and a belt. On his bare feet, he wore sandals. On his head, he wore a hat. One by one, Pastor Noble would take each of them and ask them, in regards to their confession of faith, if they believe that Jesus Christ is the Son of God, born of a virgin, died for their sins, and rose on the third day. Then, burying their old self with Christ – via submerging them below the water's surface – and raising them up anew by lifting them upward from the creek, he therein submerged them in the name of the Father, and of the Son, and of the Holy Spirit as Christ commanded, hugging each one of their necks and welcoming them into the Kingdom of GOD.

It was a touching reunion filled with love and community. Pastor Noble taught the young new converts the importance of reading their Bibles daily, as the Word of The LORD is nourishment for the souls of His Children. Moreover, he had a kind of question-and-answer session that he by no means planned or asked for, but it just kind of happened. Jackie and Penny had such a love for community, leaving no doubt that they were in the right line of work. The ministerial – like the cross – goes both ways: vertical, between man and GOD; and horizontal, from person to person. You can't just love the LORD; you have to love people too. In fact, scripture says that if you don't love your brother, whom you have seen – then you most certainly don't love GOD, whom you have not.

Penny and Jackie stopped back at the house, where he could get cleaned up a bit from all of the outdoor baptism and such. Thereafter, the two of them went to a local dinner for lunch. Once there, Jackie ordered the Salisbury steak, mashed potatoes, and green beans. Penny ordered the meatloaf, mashed potatoes, and greens. Besides this, each of them had a tall glass of sweet tea to guzzle down with their meal, which would likely be followed by a midday coffee, a slice of peach cobbler, and a scoop of vanilla ice cream.

When the coffee came and Jackie took a sip, Penny looked at him straight-faced with no expression of mirth and asked, "Good to the last drop?" To which Jackie smiled back at her sarcastically and answered, "I'll let you know." Aside from the pastor and his wife looking at each other like a bunch of love-struck school kids, as if they were unashamed for the world to know the love they had found in one another as well as in Christ, a few acquaintances said hello to them and vice versa while they were there.

Besides all of this, there is little more that could be said outside of the fact that Penny mentioned to her husband how it was good that the evangelist Harold Sizemore wasn't there, too, in the dinner to see the two of them drinking coffee, of all things. Harold was one of a number of people within the Pentecostal faith who sincerely believed that aside from alcohol, the Bible's admonition against partaking of strong drink likewise encompassed soda pops, coffee, and tea.

"Caffeine will kill you!" he'd exclaim as if hoping that the Heavens would approvingly hear him say it. It was as if drinking coffee was a sin – such as having a beer, smoking a cigarette, going to the moving picture show and watching some foul film, dancing to secular music, or what-have-you – it was Jackie's only vice. GOD knew that he'd never felt convicted of it, and if he had, he'd stop drinking coffee right then and there, just like he did with playing checkers all of those years ago. Yes, as a boy Jackie Noble was known to play two games, baseball and checkers, and he was quite good at both. Howbeit, his complete domination at the game of checkers really rang a bell with him. Many of his classmates would come and watch intently to see Jackie Noble: the boy who could not be beaten. Observing the fullness of the gameboard, he'd jump the opposing pieces one way and then another, until he began to think he'd come under conviction for it. From that day forward, Jackie hung it up and never played the game of checkers again. It was not that he didn't love it, but that he loved GOD more. Still, Penny mentioning the unlikeliness of the Reverend Harold Sizemore coming into that place, when they both knew that he wasn't in that area, was somewhat amusing.

Not to mock the man too much, Jackie did suggest that if he had the same convictions as Harold's overindulgence with the breath-freshening Sen-Sen as Harold did with his drinking coffee, the evangelist might very well have a problem with that indeed. Finishing this short but sweet statement with a light huff of air, thus causing Penny to find more humor in all of that than her playful jab before it.

After their lunch, the Nobles spend some time meditating on the LORD and making final preparations for their visitors, the Clarks. Penny had a roast going for hours in the brand-new crock pot that Jackie had bought her. She loved it so much and had already used it a number of times to make delicious, mouth-watering, gourmet meals. At present, a good-sized roast was in there, covered with diced-up carrots and onions. Besides this, she had some okra to bread and fry, some potatoes to make into mashed potatoes – but not just any mashed potatoes – her special mashed potatoes. Instead of putting milk in them, she used sour cream. They also had sautéed garlic and butter. Yet this was not yet the fullness, because unlike most mashed potatoes,Penny Noble's special mashed potatoes were whipped.

She was a woman who believed that if you were going to do something that you ought to do it right. That's why the Nobles' household didn't have a microwave like many other American homes. With a little more time an oven or stove top could reheat food and far better. One evangelist that she and her husband had heard speak even once mentioned the evils of the microwave – as within holiness churches it was pretty much within vogue to bash anything that one might even allege as worldly. At any rate, that fiery evangelist talked about how you can take a glass of water, heat it in the microwave, let it cool, and pour it on a plant, and that the plant will die. In fact, she could still hear perpetually every word of his sermon in her head…

"You know that can't be good for you! Satan is a deceiver! Know you not that your bodies are the temple of the Holy Ghost? And yet you put bad things into it. You read junk. You let your kids listen to the Devil's music, and you tell yourself that it's not affecting you – but it is affecting you. Everything affects us. Just like Samson, so many Christians want to give a little here and give a little there – but, honey, one day when the enemy is upon you and you need the Holy Ghost power of GOD in your life, you'll find out that just assuming that He is around will be assuming wrong.

My LORD, my GOD! The Bible says that I am persuaded to believe that neither death, nor life, nor angels, nor principalities, nor powers, nor things present, nor things to come, nor height, nor depth, nor any other creature, shall be able to separate us from the love of GOD! …But then I know what some of you might be saying. You might be saying wait a minute, preacher – what

else is there? If not these things, what is there that could get in between me and the most Holy GOD? Honey, it's you. You've allowed distractions to get in-between you and your relationship with Christ. You've allowed other people, circumstances, and rock music to hinder your walk.

GOD wants to put good things in you, and just like those godforsaken microwaves that they're selling in the stores – the devil wants to feel you poison – but it's not just any poison. He'll feed you sweet little lies and bring things into your life that you think are gifts from Heaven, when they come straight out of Hell. For GOD's sake – get the microwaves of worldliness out of your life and long for the bread of Heaven. Oh, taste and see that the LORD is good," he declared.

Ironically, of all people, that specific preacher who preached that sermon was the Evangelist Harold Sizemore, whom Penny had jested about being opposed to her and her husband's indulgence of drinking caffeinated coffee – or, as Harold had once called it, the Devil's brew. In fact, once, when he was rabbit-trailing off amid a sermon about the wickedness of drinking strong drink, of which coffee was the beverage of choice, he spoke at length of how bugs and other such disgusting things were ground up with the coffee beans at the processing plants. He went on so with such disparaging details that several people avowed never to drink coffee again – but not her Jackie. He said after service that while Brother Harold preached a good message, he felt more conviction as to how his sermons needed to focus more on the blood of Christ than his morning pick-me-up. Responsively, a mirthful part of her thought how just like any good shoe salesman, her

preacher-man-husband, Jackie Noble didn't like having his toes stepped on, though she was kind and clever enough to not let that jest see the light of day.

Several hours passed by, and Roger Clark's 1970 AMC Hornet Sportabout Wagon pulled into the Nobles' driveway. Stepping outside, Jackie hollered out to him,

"Boy, I sure do like that car."

Smiling, Roger called back, "Ain't she a beaut'?" Their reunion was grand. The Nobles and the Clarks both talked about old times and current events, how big little Davie was getting, as well as the school bus exorcism that took place the day before, and the baptismal service down at the creek earlier that morning.

"It sure does sound like y'all have been busy," Annette exclaimed.

"I only wish that we could do more for The LORD than we're doing right now," Penny said in response with complete sincerity and an abundance of humility.

Besides all of the good food and conversation about the general affairs of life, the two families more or less had church in some sense there inside the Noble's' quaint Georgia home. Their conversations bordered on testimonies. A few times, they all stopped to pray over this person or that person. Sometimes it was like coming at a fly with a hammer, and other prayers like coming at a giant with a sling and smooth stone. Regardless, they all believed together that GOD would give them the victory in every situation.

When Sunday morning – August 20th, 1972 – came, about the hustle that you could imagine went on for five people, as opposed to two, o get ready inside of the Noble home. At their suggestion, Jackie took little David down to the church with him, arriving well before his wife, who would be commuting with their friends, Annette and Roger.

Teaching him how to sweep, the two of them both tackled the task together. Jackie took the parking lot while Davie took the front porch. Before letting the child have at it, the kindly-hearted pastor illustrated to him how to clean all of the spider webs from in between the banisters. Also, possibly making it more amusing, was that there was a writing spider in a high-up web.

Jackie pointed up to it and told Davie, "Now, you see there?"

"Uh-huh," Davie answered.

"That's what they call a writing spider," he told him.

"What's a writing spider?" Davie asked.

"It's kind of like the spider in the book Charlotte's Web," he answered.

Then, with a worried look on his face, Davie asked Pastor Noble if he was going to kill the spider, whom he now called Charlotte. Assuring the child that he was just going to shake it off in the grass and let it trail off somewhere else, Davie's first time sweeping Soul's Harbor Holiness Church had begun.

The first of his helpers to arrive was Sister Young.

"My, what a nice young man," she said as she approached the Pastor, looking off at Davie as she said it.

"Well now, I've not been called that in a while," Jackie answered; ribbing her.

Sister Young gave him a sardonic smile, to which Jackie chucklingly told her that the boy belonged to their house guests. Right about the time that the two of them were talking, Penny, Roger, and Annette pulled up in his AMC Hornet.

Making her way over, as something of a greeting committee, Sister Young shook hands with Roger, hugged Penny and Annette, and carried on with them for a moment just outside of earshot from Jackie. As he swept the parking lot, he kind of smirked to himself, thinking how humorous he'd found his little joke moments ago. Meanwhile, Davie laid his broom aside and dashed down through the parking lot to hug his Mom and Dad, greet Penny – whom he'd likewise not seen for what was at most forty-five minutes – and carry on a conversation with Sister Young as though he'd known her for his whole life.

Roger came over to Jackie and told him how he swore how it seemed like that boy of theirs had never met a stranger. Then putting his hand firmly on Jack's shoulder, tears welled up in his eyes as he told him, "I'm so glad that we have him. Thank you."

Firmly, he embraced the pastor and began crying tears of joy, exclaiming to him in a bit more than a stage whisper how wickedly awful it is what America is doing to little children, the lies that they've spread, the lives that they've ruined. Taking a few moments to ruminate on all of this, affirming one another by citing various accounts that they and others had genuinely seen, as well as paraphrasing a small handful of scriptures in the midst of there conversation – a sound like a gunshot rang out as Brother Vincent's car backfired while turning the corner down the way, as he drove towards Souls Harbor's parking lot.

>"That right there is Brother Vincent and Sister Shirley Mayfield – you know, like the milk," Jackie told him.

>"That'll be easy to remember," Roger answered as he wiped his eyes, took out a handkerchief, and gave his nose an explosive honk in an effort to compose himself.

It was about that time that Shirley Mayfield was getting out of her car. The sneeze was so loud that everyone heard it. When she and her husband, Vincent, approached, she even commented as to how that was some sneeze; with a smile. He then asked her to excuse him and again began to rehash the horrors of the sinful act of abortion and how blessed he and his wife were.

>"I love him like my own. I don't care what anybody says; that's my boy, and I'm proud to be his dad," he said.

After that, this all naturally resolved into the six of them tidying up the church before Sunday school. It was a tumultuous time around the world. Earlier that month, the pro-life Democratic candidate for the Presidency – Governor George Wallace, a rampant segregationist who said that he planned to "out-nigger" President

Richard Milhous Nixon – was running for his second term. Alleged political violence and corruption were at an all-time high. It largely involved a series of purported coups led by President Nixon and the Republican party in a series of events known as the Watergate Scandal. There were several things had happened on May, 5th, White House operatives were arrested for burglarizing the Democratic National Committee in June, and the list of charges only went on from there. For those of the congregants who had television and/or read the papers, there was some hope that they might hear a bit of good news – that is, presuming that the representatives for America did well at the Olympics, which would begin in Munich that Saturday. Still, while any of this might be mentioned at any given time, a short but passing thought, the red-hot Georgian Sunday school teacher was far more concerned with what the Bible said than how the papers read.

He began that Sunday morning's class by announcing to everyone that he'd read the back of The Book (i.e. The Holy Bible) and we won.

"Contrary to how some people act, the unadulterated Word of GOD doesn't end with an 'OH ME' but with an 'AMEN!' I wish to GOD that somebody in this house would get happy in Jesus Christ! I wish to GOD that somebody would get up on their feet and praise him!" he exhorted in the preachiest of thunder-tones.

What was supposed to be a teaching-type lesson for them once more turned into a vivacious free-for-all. People would exclaim things like – "Where the Spirit of The LORD is, there is liberty!" One woman testified about how she used to dance at the honky-tonks when she was in the world and then went on to say how she's still

dancing – but that she's changed partners. To that, some brother – who was delivered of alcoholism – exclaimed how when he was in the world, he used to drink and then added that now he's drinking from a different tap. He then began talking about that Living Water that we read about in scripture, but before he could finish, he broke out into a Pentecostal Holy Ghost jig – which to those who'd never seen such a thing could be described as looking most reminiscent to a non-stationary form of clogging or buckboard dancing.

Then, at some point during the Sunday school service, which had once more turned into full-blown church, Sister Betty Sue Riley began playing that piano in the Pentecostal way. The song was one that everybody knew: "That's Him." It was a favorite of hers, and when she began to play it and sing it, that song soothed her soul.

THAT'S HIM

VERSE 1
If you meet a stranger – on the Jericho road
That's Him - That's Him
If He walks beside you – Freely sharing your load
That's Him - That's Him

CHORUS
That's Him - My savior don't you know
This Man of Galilee – Whose blood availed for me
If He fills – Your cup to the brim
That's Him - That's Him

VERSE 2
If somebody calls you in the still of the night
That's Him - That's Him
If you feel a yearning for a life that is right
That's Him - That's Him

It genuinely seemed like the Holy Spirit was trying to usher revival into Souls Harbor Holiness Church. The mighty moving of the presence of GOD was so tangible that, at times, it looked as though a thick, humid mist or film was in the air around them. Moreover, something seemingly was happening in the life of Jackie Noble which had become somewhat evident due to the exorcism that'd taken place two days before, as well as the prayerful and baptismal conversions of several young people. In his heart he wondered if any of those teens would be in service with them on this glorious Sunday, or off fellowshipping with their families or possibly friends who'd, long before he met them, brought this about by an abundance of prayer that the principalities, powers, and rulers of darkness enacting a stronghold against those gods could no longer delay.

Like an accumulative filling of a bowl, those prayers began also to fill a golden bowl in Heaven until it could hold no more and like a mighty crashing wave devastated the forces of darkness that sought to keep salvation from them. After taking up prayer requests and the people worshiping in their giving of tithes and offerings unto the LORD, Sister Annette Clark was introduced and came up to the platform. With tears in her eyes, she testified as to how powerfully she felt the Spirit of The LORD moving in the midst of them. Then she began to sing a relatively new song that was released by The Gaither Trio the previous year entitled: "Something Beautiful." It meshed with her testimony extremely well.

With no lack of detail, she told the congregation in plain terms that any adult could understand – all while keeping the darker affairs over the heads of the younger children by the choice of words – of how terrible her young life was. She told of the lack of love, support, and

hope that she had until she came to Jesus Christ. Certainly, Annette had known a few people who claimed to be Christians prior to this. They even went to church, but when she needed love, they weren't there. Then, at the end of her rope, she – a young pregnant lady whose family all but outright rejected her – was going to terminate her pregnancy inside the abortion clinic. That's when she met Penny Noble.

Annette shared the love and care that she was shown by the Nobles, and expressed that she couldn't imagine how hard all of that must have been for them, being a newlywed couple themselves. Yet, they took her in like she was family. It was like they had known her all of her life. They didn't just preach to her in words but also in how they lived. She saw Jesus Christ living inside of them. Before ever really reading the Bible, they were the Bible that she read. She expressed the utmost of gratitude for them.

As she made an end to all of what she was saying, with teary eyes, she then reprised the chorus to the song written by Bill and Gloria Gaither that she'd started with. She sang:

"Something Beautiful – Something Good
All my confusion – He understood
All I had to offer Him was brokenness and strife
But He made something beautiful of my life."

From thenceforth, Sister Annette made something of a hand gesture to her husband, Roger, which was apparently his queue to come up to the platform and say something into the microphone to the congregation. Affirming what she'd just said, he told the story of his own life, how he was a widower, and how the Nobles had brought her to church. There was a great deal of

sweetness and romance to all that he said. He quoted passages of scripture like:

"What God hath joined together, let no man separate." (MARK 10:9) *Speaking of the unity of marriage. "...a threefold chord is not quickly broken." (ECCLESIASTES 4:12) *in relation to the unity of a marital covenant that is harmoniously in relational covenant with GOD. Many people found the personality and vulnerability found within this couple's testimonies moving. They thanked them. Some folks even said that the next time they came to that church, they'd no longer be mere visitors, adding how the lot of them were family.

Roger, Annette, and Davie wouldn't be in service with Souls Harbor Holiness Church that evening. They'd be making tracks back home before work Monday morning. The Nobles, Clarks, and a few other families all came together at the local buffet to share a meal and further fellowship. Roger had already packed everything up before they came down to the church with Sister Penny that morning. Now, the only thing between the Nobles and that Sunday evening's service was a midday nap.

Jackie's mind raced – hashing and rehashing his initial meeting with Henry and George, the conversation in the shoe department, the school bus exorcism, and the somewhat impromptu baptismal service that followed. None of the young people from any of that were with their congregation that Sunday morning. Inwardly, the pastor wondered when he'd see them again.

That evening at Souls Harbor Holiness Church, things began normally enough, or rather normal for their congregation. Turning into the Red Back Hymnal – which is also commonly known as the Church of GOD Hymnal, as it is published by the Church of GOD Cleveland Assembly, Inc. – they began by singing some familiar songs. The hymns sung that evening were as follows:

- I Love to Walk with Jesus
- I Shall Not Be Moved
- Keep on the Firing Line
- Heaven's Jubilee
- I Never Shall Forget the Day

As usual, their regular pianist, Betty Sue Riley, walked up in a passive manner and began to play while Sister Martha dictated the next page number and subsequent hymn to follow. Yessir, it was a hand-clapping, foot-stomping time, indeed. A few people gave some brief testimonies as to how good GOD had been to them. Others talked about how blessed they felt by the things shared that morning. After all of this, the opportunity to worship in their giving through tithes and offerings, prayer requests, as well as a call to shake hands and welcome everyone around them, it finally came time for Pastor Noble to deliver the word of The Lord. Whereas he also doubled as the church's guitarist, he was typically seated on a pulpit throughout the fullness of each service. And it was because of this that he was able to be so ultra observant to the things going on in the pews: who walked in, who walked out, and the like.

Amid the regulars, he saw that two young people who were at the Saturday morning baptism had come in and took a seat near the back during the end of the song service. As he approached the podium, he thanked everyone there and made a series of declarations for the sake of the newly converted, unlearned youths – one of which was the Bible's teaching that where the Spirit of The LORD is there is liberty to worship.

After these things, he turned to the key text for the evening, the singular verse James 4:7, which reads: "Submit yourselves therefore to God. Resist the devil, and he will flee from you."

After reading the verse, Pastor Noble began to contextually tell the congregants about those things written directly around it. The preceding six verses talked about how the people within the body of believers were lustful, adulterous, and bound themselves to things and persons contrary to the faith that they walked in. The verses that followed likewise called them to purify themselves and rebukingly called the church audience that these words were written for the double-minded. Like any competent minister, Pastor Noble felt that all of these statements, in direct correspondence with the verse that he'd afore-read, were points to be expounded upon.

"Now, you may ask me – Preacher, why is it that the Devil doesn't flee from me? And I'd say right back to you, Have you submitted yourself to GOD? The reason that devils aren't intimidated by so many so-called Christians is because so many of us have more in common with the demons than we do the heavenly Father. It's like Jesus told Simon Peter. Jesus said to him, Get thee behind me Satan – but He didn't just stop at calling him Satan. No-siree-bob! Jesus explained it. Jesus called Simon Peter 'Satan' – a name used in scripture for both a type of demon and as a definite article, that means adversary – because Peter cared more for the things of the world than for the things of GOD.

Is it any wonder why Jesus preached, 'Blessed are the poor in spirit'? It sounds backwards, doesn't it? There are people all through life that are chasing one cheap high and then another. Some do it through materialism. Think of Judas Iscariot. The major turning point in his story was when he saw this woman, Mary, give extravagant praise to the LORD Jesus Christ. The perfumed oil that she anointed Him with was the only thing of this world that Christ brought with Him to the cross. Judas valued money more than Judas valued GOD, and just like him, this world is filled with people who try to find peace in the material things, only to be empty five minutes later until the next big thing comes along. Are you chasing after GOD or earthly possessions?

Jesus also said, 'Blessed are they that mourn.' But how does that sound? We live in a world filled with people who are wanting to be affirmed by this person and that person all of their lives. If they can just pat them on the head and tell them how pleased they are as that sad individual twists and bends themselves every which way to make everyone happy but the LORD of all creation. Friends, I'm here to tell you that the kind of person that I'm speaking of would be better off spiritually if they weren't so concerned with the opinions of other men, but rather that they submitted their lives to the holy GOD who made them."

As he preached, several congregants got happy, whooping and hollering out "yes" and "amen!" throughout the sanctuary. Then, eventually, his personal detailed account of what happened Friday evening and, thereafter, on Saturday morn – with the exclusion of mentioning the reporter from the newspaper – was told unto them.

"It was a dark and shadowy place in the backwoods somewhere. If I had to journey back there again, I don't know that I could find it. The sun was still in the sky, but shadows hung in that place with a secular sort of blackness. In fact, some of the blackness was the blackest black that I'd ever seen before. Have any of you ever seen something blacker than black?

A crowd began to gather and I got onto the bus – but, honey, I didn't go alone – I had the Holy Ghost with me. When a demon spirit spoke out of that young man that day, it stepped into a battle that was the LORD's to fight. Now, let me tell you something you oughta know about fighting with GOD. There's really only two things:

#1) You can't win.

#2) GOD can't lose.

Church, we are admonished to put on the whole armor of GOD, that we might be able to stand against the wiles of The Devil. For we wrestle not against flesh and blood, but against principalities, against powers, against the rulers of darkness, and spiritual wickedness in high places! The weapons of our warfare are not carnal, but mighty through GOD in the pulling down of strongholds; casting down imaginations and every high thing that exalteth itself against the knowledge of GOD!

But you tell me, 'Preacher, we've never even come into contact with a demon.' And I'll answer back, 'Honey, maybe you have – maybe I have, but they hid themselves, cause they see us as no real threat.' Devils popped up all the time in the presence of Jesus. But they feel comfortable around most so-called Christians today because we have more in common with them than we do with Christ," Pastor Noble fervently exclaimed.

After all of these sayings, he thereby exclaimed with all boldness how he issued a challenge unto the forces of darkness to come out and fight. Perhaps he no more than anyone else expected an on-the-spot answer, yet that is exactly what they received. With her hair cast down in such a way that it was over her face, a sister sitting in the pews began to buckle at the knees spasmodically and rolled her head around in an orbiting pattern, while her shoulders moved something like a twitchy salsa dance. The overall contortions of the woman – who was halfway kneeling and halfway in a crab walk pose – were in similitude to the demonized young man on the school bus from days before.

"Leave us alone, Servant of the Most High GOD," the gravelly and masculine voice said from out of the woman.

Responsively, the pastor engaged the demon, telling it to come out. Howbeit, unlike the seemingly lesser thing on the bus, this demon or demons refused to be expelled so easily. And thus the wrestling match – as he'd as much called it – by way of scripture ensued. Verses were quoted one after another, saying such things as, "Let GOD arise and His enemies be scattered. Let them that hate Him flee before Him. As the wax is melted away by the flame so perish the wicked in the

presence of GOD. Also, when the enemy comes rushing in – like a flood GOD raises up a standard against it" – and so on and so forth.

During their bout – which lasted for a good 45 minutes there for everyone in the church to see and hear – the devil inside of this woman, who even then bent and malformed her face, making her unrecognizable from the sister they knew and loved – spoke of how it had been with her for a long time. From out of her mouth it told of how her father had come up to her room and molested and beat her over and over again all throughout her childhood. Likewise, this vile thing told about how her husband was a kindred spirit to her dad and that is why she was drawn to him. She was tied to the abuse. This demon told the pastor that he had his assignment and that nobody was about to stop him from that.

Besides all of this, the woman's hands nervously began to wipe down her arms in a way that projected stress. They too caressed her breasts in a circular seductive manner, running all around her sides, stomach, and at times up her thighs. She slid around on the floor, being dragged around by this foul thing that puppeteered her. As the skirt of her dress continually slid up further, this demon spoke crude sexual things to the pastor, men, and even women of the congregation in regards to how it wished that they'd all come now and have intercourse with this wretched soul. The whole time people were praying – and mostly at a distance. Two men and three other women within their church body help restrain her from stripping off her clothes. One brought a blanket to cover the lower portion of her body, as the bottom of her dress was now closing in on her hip region.

Profanities and endless spewings of lewdness came out of the creature through her. This thing mocked her and reveled in her misery, brokenness, and every drop of abuse that she'd endured. It took every bit of the two men's strength, each of whom held down one of her arms with all of his might to keep her still. Before this, she'd tore off nearly half of the top buttons of her dress open, which caused it to be opened just a bit below the bottom of her ivory-colored brazier. Finally, after ceaseless prayers, invoking the power of Jesus' name and calling that bestial thing inside of her to go down into the pit, she thereafter became very still.

Many apologies were given on her part, and tears were shed. In part, she seemed to be unaware of what had happened, while in other ways she felt completely humiliated by the scene that was made. Trying to give her ease, the few that were with her told her that the LORD had set her free. One of them even explained how it sounded like a door had been opened in her life that she had nothing directly to do with, and now thankfully that door was shut. Words cannot do justice to describe the atmosphere within the sanctuary of Souls Harbor Holiness Church that night. While a miraculous deliverance had taken place, this was not received with the same spirit that a cripple getting out of their wheelchair or a blind person opening their eyes to see for the first time. This was something far different.

Jackie Noble had worked in the power and authority of the Holy Spirit through the name of Jesus, in the perfect will of The Father, as prescribed in the holy scripture, to vanquish demonic evil, and yet no one shouted around the church, clapped, or sang praises to the King of Kings. What had begun as a lewd and profanely violent demonic manifestation had now turned into a time of solemnity and perceivable contemplation in the hearts and minds of some. The disheveled woman held the pastor, all while at the same time using her other hand to keep the top of her blouse closed.

Jackie, Penny, and Sister Young helped her to her car, becoming all the more aware, as she brushed her hair from out of her face, that this was Betty Sue Riley – their church's piano player. As she wheeled off, Sister Young said as much.

"Why, I never knew she had a life quite like that," she added.

The darkness has a way of creeping in through any nook and cranny it can. If an open door is not available, it would gladly come through a window. Several people hung around and talked, dispelling from the place like dandelion petals in the breeze. Many of them looked dumbstruck. Shock and awe would be a fairly accurate way of summing the whole affair up.

Tears of thanksgiving trickled down Jackie and Penny Noble's faces as they praised the LORD for setting their sister free. He'd issued a challenge unto the devil, and while a battle had been won that Sunday evening, the war had just begun. A young teenage lady and her friend who was comparable in age both expressed to the pastor how they really thought that was something. He wondered whether the two of those girls might think that his church or ministry had always been like this. Still, his response went more to the effect of telling them that just like GOD was great inside of the burning bush – GOD was great inside of him. GOD didn't make the bush great, but GOD was great in the bush.

Just like that, he thought of how GOD would keep metaphorical birds of the air from lighting upon him. He thought of how likewise, no metaphorical parasites of bugs might chip away at him. That all-consuming fire within would leave behind only white ash while the bush remained unharmed as a baby chick beneath the safety of its mother's wing. All was well as he supposed.

Monday morning – August 21st, 1972 – came along, and after having a refreshing cup of his favorite coffee, Jackie sped off in his station wagon to the J.C. Penny shoe department for what he thought would be just another average day of work. Mondays had always been an anomaly. In Genesis, it was the only day that GOD didn't pronounce as being good. This is largely because on the second day – which we commonly call by the pagan name Monday – GOD himself separated The Deep. Within the Bible ancient mythologies, and near-eastern literature alike, The Deep, or rather The Sea, is a treacherous place, emblematic of darkness, the abyss, a lurking evil, and Hell. It was home to that great sea monster Leviathan.

This is why GOD could never call this day good – as it dealt specifically with evil. When writing the account of Genesis, Moses even went to great lengths to demythologize the text. Never once did he say that GOD created the Sun and the Moon as those were the names of their neighboring countries' gods. Rather, he said that GOD created a light to rule by day and a lesser light to rule by night. Simply put, GOD did not create evil – evil is just a perversion of something that was otherwise good. Evil is something where the light of GOD's goodness does not reside. Thereby, our words that point away from GOD can be evil. Places, activities, bad relationships, and even those things that masquerade as church, yet are not, can be evil. Evil is not evil for its own sake; it just tries to get favorable or right-seeming results in the wrong way. Thereby it is corrupted. Thereby it is evil. And with this point well made, nearly fifteen minutes after Jackie had left for work, the Nobles' phone began to ring.

The call that Penny received was from Gertrude Miller, a woman whose nagging voice was easily discernible to perceive. Immediately, she began to talk about the service, hours before. While much of it began with complementary things being said of the pastor's preaching, Gertrude then segued into the real reason that she was calling: to discuss how queer of a thing it seemed to her that their very own sister – Betty Sue Riley – had been possessed by a demon for all of those years.

"It was plumb indecent," she ranted.

"I was ashamed at the stories that woman told in mixed company and in the presence of children," she added.

"Did you see the things that she was doing to her body? Did you see her hands and how she was trying hard to run them up to the top of her legs? That woman must be crazy or something! It's just not right," she also added.

Every moment that it seemed like Penny was about to get a chance to say anything – like a bulldozer, Sister Gertrude pressed on through.

There was no love in Gertrude's conversation, no sympathy, or understanding. She merely reviled the poor woman, who'd secretly suffered a life of pain and abuse. Quite clearly, Betty Sue's only refuge had been the church. The house of GOD was her only soft place to land, and here, Sister Gertrude – a strong-willed woman

who was set in her ways – reviled their fellow sister in the faith, whom Jesus Christ had set free. After enduring far too much of this inflamed ranting, backbiting, and such for far longer than she wished to bear, Penny Noble butted in with a – "Now you listen right here!" – and proceeded to give Gertrude a piece of her mind.

While her conversation and her tone was tempered appropriately, Gertrude by no means would receive it that way, nor had the woman ever seemed to receive any opinion outside of her own at all. The 45-minute phone conversation ended with Gertrude expelling a – "Well, I never have heard such a thing. I would have never thought I'd hear such talk out of you." Thereafter, a bell-like dig made it clear that the woman had hung up her phone on the pastor's wife without so much as the cordiality of a goodbye. It did little to better the mood that this conversation had got her in.

Penny imagined all of the fires that might be caused by this one woman's tongue, and how she'd have to do work to put them out. When Jackie came home – she thought how she'd tell him. This was no passing thing. On their Wednesday night service, Betty Sue was not at church. Sister Gertrude acted distant, and her piercing gaze was more akin to a glare until one focused on her. Quickly adjusting her look – as one might a mask that slipped – she'd then appear more even toned. That Thursday morning, Penny called Sister Betty Sue Riley in an effort to check up on her but received no answer. On Wednesday night service, before she had heard from a few other ladies that they saw Betty Sue working the checkout line at the grocery store and she acted sunny, like she'd had a weight lifted off of her, and yet she was not in service that night. And while there could be any one of a thousand reasons that

their faithful sister and piano player was out, Penny began to pray for her friend and wonder.

Oh, how greatly it does impact a worship service when one of the musicians is out. And while this had little to nothing to do with Jackie and Penny's very real concern with for Betty, it was for those reasons all the more obvious that she was not there.

On Friday, August 25th, 1972, after Jackie left for work, Penny would receive another phone call worth mentioning. Sister Rita called to ask her if she'd seen in the newspaper that morning that there was a story about Pastor Jackie exorcizing a demon spirit out of a young drug addict, winning him and other youths to Christ, and baptizing them in the creek last weekend. Penny, unable to keep from smiling, was happy to hear of this good news. As she saw it, this dramatic story could only bring glory and honor to the name of the LORD. In response to this, Rita told her that she'd bet that Brother Dale would be all too happy to get them a copy and bring it over to the house.

"That'd be wonderful," Penny agreed in the utmost of jovial tones.

All the while, she likewise couldn't imagine that someone amidst her husband's coworkers at the J.C. Penny hadn't read the article as well. And the fact of the matter was that her feminine instincts were right.

All throughout the day, people would want to come along conversing about their own Jackie Noble casting out a demon. Some less observant people who knew him only as a shoe salesman said how they didn't know that he was a preacher. It became a testimonial witness, Sunday school lesson, and sermon of sorts as he actively recounted to them how Jesus Christ had cast out devils, the early church had cast out devils, and the Gospel of Mark ended in commissioning the followers of Christ to preach the Gospel to every living creature and, of course, cast out demons. Significantly, within the ministry of Jesus Christ, he brought nothing new, but that he had such authority to cast out demons.

The Old Testament prophets had healed people and raised the dead. The prophet Elisha even did a miracle by multiplying bread and loaves in the fourth chapter of 2nd Kings, foreshadowing what Christ would do on two different occasions on a larger scale. Jesus Christ's first miracle recorded in the Gospel of Mark was His exorcism of a demon in a synagog. After that, scripture tells us that He went all throughout the region's synagogues to expel other demons. Those people, like the majority of people who Christ healed, were Jews. They likely lived far better lives than both pagan society and many modern Christians today – yet a supernatural doorway had been opened, giving demons the legal right to inhabit these afflicted people. Whereas Pastor Jackie would explain some of this to those who seemed genuinely interested in the subject, inwardly he reflected on the long-fought years of tormentive spiritual abuse that had been inflicted on his dear sister Betty Sue.

That evening, Jackie drove home from work with entirely too much on his mind to tell and three copies of the newspaper in the seat beside him. When he slipped into the house instead of a, "Honey, I'm home," Jackie shouted,

"Look what The LORD has done!"

Stepping out of the kitchen, Penny waved her copy of the paper at him as he held three of them, which he waved at her. They both smiled and laughed.

"...so, I guess that you read the article," he said.

"Oh, yes. In fact, a lot of people have. The telephone has been ringing all day long," she answered.

"Is that so?" he responded.

"If I'm lying – I'm dying," Penny said back with a grin.

In such a manner, their conversation would continue until the phone rang, cutting through the atmosphere like a knife.

"Probably another fan," Penny jested.

"I'll get this one" Jackie told her, unaware that this was no simple recognition of praise, but a desperate call for help.

Jackie Noble was the real deal. The real gospel was conveyed through power and authority, not just weighty words, and the person on the other line knew it. They knew that GOD didn't answer everyone's prayers the same. Any fool could see that in the Bible. They needed a true Man of GOD – who was aligned with the will of The Father to come to their rescue. While neither they nor their family had ever been to Souls Harbor Holiness Church, they did just read about what he did for that demonized boy on the dilapidated school bus and had the faith to think – couldn't GOD use him to give us the miracle that we need?

It was one of those conversations that was both long and short all at the same time. Just by observing the preacher, Penny could tell that whatever was being said – it was intense. This all seemed such a strange thing to them, and yet at the same time, who was to say that this was not the hand of the LORD? When Jackie got off the phone, he told Penny that immediately after finishing their meal he wanted to take her down to the address he'd scrawled on a piece of paper, as dictated to him by the person on the other line.

"It appears that this exorcist does house calls," he said, and then shoveled a bite of mashed potatoes in his mouth.

CHAPTER 08

An Exorcistic House Call

Since this whole thing started with all of the oddness of the school-bus exorcism, a progression of events had come about that seemed to indicate that GOD was really trying to do something in this community and that the Nobles were His chosen vessels to do it. Now here Pastor Jackie and Penny went in his '68 station wagon to an address that was just over an hour's drive away. While neither he nor his wife had ever met the person that he spoke to on the other end of the phone, they sounded desperate. As Jackie finished eating his supper, he'd gone through something of an explanation, which was to be continued along their ride.

With that, at the drop of the hat, the two got themselves together, Jackie laid hold on his leather-bound King James Bible – the same Bible that bore his name upon the lower right-hand corner of the cover. It had actually been a gift from his dear friend and mentor, the Reverend Doctor Byron Phillips, from his days serving as the youth pastor at New Life Fellowship Church. It was for this reason that his name bore the title "Pastor" on it. It was precious to him and – having several – this was the Bible that he'd used ever since that time and carried in to preach as a pastor at Souls Harbor Holiness Church.

The pages were worn from much reading. Words were underlined in red, blue, or black ink, with some phrases and even whole sentences being circled. Along the top, bottom, and side margin he'd very carefully written small notes about one thing or another in as brief of a way as possible. Anyone who might open it and look within its pages – even ignoring the personalized cover – would easily deduce that this was a minister's Bible, and one who took it all very seriously.

As the two of them journeyed this distance, it also seemed ideal that they get some coffee for the added energy that might be needed. Subsequently, swinging by a fast-food drive-through window, Penny and Jackie got themselves cups of black coffee, and on they went.

The household that they were visiting was something like theirs, in its own way. The couple was married, had no children, and this fellow believed in the power of prayer. The man whom Jackie had spoken with told him that he'd read the article in the newspaper and felt an urgency to track down his telephone number and plead for his help. After all, the man suggested – how many preachers do you hear that go around casting out demons – he'd asked him. The truth was, it was sinfully rare, especially among of the Pentecostal, Church of GOD, Assemblies of GOD, Independent Holiness churches, and such who believed in the active manifestation of the power of the Holy Ghost working and moving through the saints until that which is perfect – Jesus Christ – returns in the clouds of glory to call both the living and dead who belong to Him home. Still, in spite of this, the largest church within all of Christendom to perform exorcism rights was the Catholic Church. In fact, at one point they even had an office for individuals called exorcists.

While within the supernatural, a real witch might rather notably have the ability to transfer demons from one person or thing to another by invoking hexes, spells, or the like, it was only by the sovereign power of Almighty GOD in the mighty name of Jesus Christ that they could be cast out of someone or something. And while getting them out was one thing, keeping them out was another. Really it was all a part of the same process, though. The Holy Ghost-filled believer – whether a preacher or not – would lead the individual to renounce and denounce any such thing that had given those devils a foothold to come into them in the first place. Sometimes it would be a generational curse passed down from one family member to another. Other times, repetitively committing the same sinful act over and over again would open a door. Then sometimes trauma or abuse would do it – and thereby, Jackie would come to find out that asking questions – just like a competent lawyer or physician, as perhaps both professions were somewhat applicable in a spiritual sense concerning the matters of diabolical possession, diabolical vexation, diabolical obsession, or even perhaps diabolical infestation – which is the one thing of these that deals with a place being afflicted by the demonic rather than a person – was the way to deduce exactly what course needed to be taken to bring restoration to the troubled soul.

And with all of that said, Jackie Noble had not yet contended with any of these other things. In both cases before, as well as the home that he and his wife journeyed to, these were all clear-cut cases of diabolical possession, which is to have a demonic presence of one or more being inside of a person, affecting, and influencing them. The demon might also drive them to sin or influence others to do terrible things to that individual. After all, they feed on the filth and ungodliness of this world. Some might propel the person whom they have hold over to take drugs, consume alcohol, look at pornography, perform self-gratification, have adulterous affairs, lie excessively, mindlessly swear, and so forth. Moreover, they attracted the worst sorts – which is highly observable even by the nonreligious.

Why does the girl who was abused by her father marry a man just like him? Everything works this way. A kindred spirit, whether good or evil, allures one person to another. Within Christendom, our spirits are to bear witness, one with another. Within sin, various indulgences that hold little more than a momentary pleasure until the next fix are endlessly pursued as the wayward fool seeks to fill the hole inside of them that only GOD himself can fill.

In his mind's eye, Pastor Jackie day-dreamt that he and his wife, Penny, arrived at what best could be described to appear as a 1930s-looking two-story house in the black of night. Pulling into the driveway and stepping from the car, he then rounded over to the other side to gentlemanly open the door for his wife. Both in the natural and in this dream, they'd prayed on the way there and were praying still.

"LORD, in the glorious name of Jesus Christ we pray that you'd have the power of the Holy Ghost to come upon us like never before. We pray that we can be an encouragement to this family and set this woman free. We pray that peace will come to this household. Evil has no authority here. We come against it in Jesus name…" Jackie prayed.

Likewise, Penny alongside him was praying a non-mechanical prayer. Their words jumbled together, the ones with the others, and as they prayed everything around them seemed to change in a way that they could feel down deep within their souls. Jackie was encouraged. Coming in with a record of 2-0 – and serving an all-powerful GOD, who simply could not be beat – gave him the utmost of confidence as he stepped forth in this fabricated illusion of his mind, all while at the same time watching the road and traveling onward towards the real situation of which he only now imagined.

There in his mind's eye, as well as in reality, he and his beloved wife stepped out into darkness as emissaries of The Light. Thus the two of them walked from the driveway along the sidewalk that led up to the couple's front porch. Jackie knocked, Penny stood beside him, and then they waited.

Suddenly, the Holy Ghost-filled and highly caffeinated pastor discernibly heard a blood-curdling scream erupt from the house that stood before them, such as one might expel if they were in the deepest states of agony. Doubtlessly, the voice, while muffled, was a woman's, and while there was no beauty to the raking of it, her vocals fell somewhere in the alto range. Aside from the screaming was an array of maddening profanity, with pronouns like, "You son of a" this or "mother" that. The raging woman's favorite of the swear words – and yes, she did use them all and in repetition – had four letters in it and began with the letter "F." She'd yell, F*** this and F*** that. The strange verb which some within academia had suggested to have initially been an acronym for:

Fornicate
Under
Consent of the
King.

Every vile word ejecting out of her mouth could be heard. This sickening, supernatural stink of the demonic permeated this place from out of her, lifting its way up to Heaven. With no argument within him, Jackie felt completely assured that this would be the night that this family would be set free. However this all came to happen, the crude-sounding woman was saying them over and over again with the intention of being vile, thus conveying to the pastor that she either had a demon indeed, was a crude unwholesome individual, or had a problem with rage, or perhaps something else. These hypotheses all tethered on the assumption that she wasn't being tortured by some maniac who'd aimed to also lead the preacher and his wife into a trap. Turning the doorknob, within this strange vision of anticipated conflict, the reverend stuck his head in and called out,

"Hello! It's the preacher that you called. I have my wife with me. Can we be of some assistance?"

Before the man to whom he'd spoken could answer, the woman swearing profusely more or less hollered that the minister and his wife – both of whom she disparaged in the most explicit of ways – told them what they could do with themselves, and thereby essentially suggested that they both leave. Both after this and through the fog of hysterical swearing, the pastor heard her husband's voice calling them to come upstairs – then everything grew strangely, yet thankfully quiet.

Jackie Noble hated the very sound of profanity. It was the language spoken by filth and falls who knew no other. As Christ taught, whatsoever cometh out of a man defiles him, for from out of the heart the mouth speaks. GOD knew that he'd heard enough of it growing up. Jackie's childhood was in anything but a Christian home. His daddy was a drunk and his momma was just some kind of plain, ordinary-variety sinner. They'd have friends over, or at least what they'd call friends. Jackie was invited to a Vacation Bible School down at an area Pentecostal Church. It was about a mile and a quarter distance from where they lived. Every day of it that year, as a young seven-year-old boy, Jackie would attend. It's where he had a genuine come-to-Jesus moment. It was there at an old-fashioned altar where he gave his heart to Christ. They say it's not how hard you shout and dance inside the church but how you walk when you're six feet from the door that determines whether you're saved or not.

And such was the case of Jackie Noble. He'd heard the ugliest generalized cussing – cussing church, and cussing the LORD – as a small child than anyone ever could in their whole life. He'd have to step over the sleeping bodies of sops and wash the vomit out of the bathtub most Sundays to even get up and go to church. Nobody would make him anything for breakfast, so he'd generally either have some white bread, pick a tomato off the vine on his way to worship, or go without. When he heard cussing like that, whether in real life or a dream, it reminded him of where he came from. His daddy didn't believe in him. His daddy mocked him when as a little boy he said that The Holy Ghost had called him to be a minister of The LORD Jesus Christ. And yet, here he was still with it: determined, faithful, blessed of GOD, called, anointed, appointed, ordained, and a known enemy of the forces of darkness. Yessir, every time he heard swearing like he'd heard in this vision it reminded him of that.

As he journeyed onward into this nightmare dreamscape, abruptly, the husbandman upstairs with his wife began a hysterical discourse of his own, which in some essence sounded prayerful and in another way, blasphemous. And thus it came.

"Oh, Dear GOD up in Heaven! Oh, GOD! GOD, is she dead! Oh, my GOD! Jesus! Jesus, help me! Oh, my GOD – please help me. Dear GOD, help me!" the husband's voice cried out in some sort of terror – with a few expletives added to what he said.

Amid all of this, Jackie made his way to the top of the stairs. All the while, he continued to jointly pray with an elevated tone as if attempting to overtake the profane spirit that saturated this home's atmosphere. Everything in the upstairs of the two-story house was torn apart. Picture frames were hanging lopsided, knocked off of walls. Flower vases which once held dirt, water, and foliage were dispelled along the floor. It was like a violent ill wind had swept over this place: replacing Godly order with demonic chaos; and the spirit of love, joy, and peace with sheer terror. There in the hallway, a nightstand had been tossed – maybe several times from out of a bedroom – into one wall, the ceiling, the floor and then another wall several times over. Certainly, the broken drywall, scratches, scuffs, and so forth implied as much.

As he journeyed onward, Penny lagged behind at a safe distance and in accordance to his instruction. In this oh-too-real imagination of his, Jackie began to wonder why he'd brought his wife, all while at the same

time, he knew no one whose faith he trusted more. In this place, lamps had been knocked over and the indentations of someone's fist had been beaten into the walls, which also had deep-set claw marks from what he presumed to be human fingernails. This was all like something out of a horror writer's nightmares. It was the type of thing that might inspire their next evil book or filthy movie. Yet from the perspective that Jackie saw it through – although be it a dream while he was yet awake – it seemed all the more personal. After all, this encounter wasn't something that would happen, but this vision was in anticipation for what would happen sooner and sooner as they came closer to the house.

The whole upstairs looked like a brawl and/or raid had taken place. Finally entering the bedroom, he found the man leaning over his wife as if in deep sorrow. Jackie Noble beheld everything. The demonized and now possibly dead woman's body lay rigged and still on the floor in an unnatural position there in the middle of what could most easily be described as carnage. Bent and contorted, her grime-ridden form was covered with scratches and seemed to be either bleeding or covered with coagulated blood. Moreover, the foul stench of vomit and feces had filled the place from the moment Jackie and his wife entered, and only now had it become apparent as to why – for in this room, she'd written all manner of vile abominable sayings and sacrilegious upon the walls with her own waste.

Covering his mouth and nose, due to the poor quality of the air, Jackie quietly muttered prayers beneath his breath as whispers as he took all of this in. The light in there was low and dim. Just like in the school bus, the demons like to hide. They like to lurk in the shadows, and they don't tend to come out of their hole until either they (#1) have to for feeling threatened by the true power of Almighty GOD, or (#2) feel it is safe to do so. Certainly, there are likewise drugs, alcohol, music, rituals, and other things that can stir them. Considering all of these things, Jackie Noble questioned what kind of Hellishness this was that he'd walked into. Then, boldly trying to take firm hold on the conversation, he prayed aloud for all to hear, at the same time trying to overcome the ghastly stench that filled this place.

"LORD, in the mighty name of Jesus Christ who has all power and authority in Heaven and on Earth, we pray that you'd reach your mighty hand down into this place and touch this situation. We call on you, Oh, LORD of Host; The LORD of the armies of Heaven. Send your holy angels to aid us in this. Feel this place with deliverance and resurrection power…" he said – and then stopped as in the real world, this visionary imagination was interrupted by his dear wife telling him that according to the directions, this next street on the left was where the couple lived.

"Here it is. It's this next road on the left. Then we're there," Penny told him.

Jarred out of it, as he had not been from her previous directions that his body mechanically responded to, he was now in the present.

"I've just been sitting here praying for the glory and the presence of GOD to be with us as never before," she told him, followed by asking if he was alright.

Jackie assured her that he was amped up and ready. All the while, they went slowly down the street, counting down unto the address they were given.

Unlike in his dream, the house was a nice one-story ranch build, sitting in a more country-town atmosphere than the suburban life he had imaged. Pulling into the driveway, he and his wife stopped, joined hands, and prayed together. Jackie had his Bible with him. Likewise, Penny announced to him that she had a small bottle of anointing oil in her purse – which in this case was extra virgin olive oil that the church had prayed over. Like in his dream, Jackie, as he so often did, rounded the car to gentlemanly open the door for his darling wife, and the two of them approached the house – this spiritual battlefield together. Yet, unlike the dream, there was no explosive screaming, the sound of breaking glass, nor anything discalming. Rather, it all seemed entirely too normal.

Just before reaching the front porch, a clean-cut younger gentleman opened his front door and then screen door, inviting the two of them to come in. He knew that it was late and had brewed some coffee. While he did not know exactly what to expect, it has always been presentable and rude not to offer a guest in one's home something to eat or drink. In all politeness, Penny and Jackie both accepted the man's offer. Penny took hers with some milk in it. Jackie always drank his coffee black.

Explaining that his wife was in the other room, the man began to tell the pastor how she'd been tormented. He said that she claimed to see shadowy figures following her. She even woke him during the night, saying that one of them had been on her, clenching her by the throat and touching her in a sexual way. He told him how she was so afraid and how this had been happening for months, and how at first he didn't believe her, but then more and more strange things kept happening that she'd attribute to demon spirits. Once more thanking them for coming, he emphasized how desperate they were for help. And while this dialogue sounds short – it was told in such a way that lasted about an hour and twenty minutes total. The first fifteen minutes was just the husband talking, then his wife – who looked and acted completely normal – entered the room and shook Penny and Jackie's hands; then she and her husband went back and forth talking about it, answering Rev. Noble's questions, and so forth.

Both of the Nobles showed so much care and compassion for the two of them. With his eyes open, Pastor Noble began to pray against any evil that was trying to lay claim on this woman and her household. Both of them had been in church as children. One thing had led to another, and they just hadn't been in a long time. Thus the pastor talked to them about having a real relationship and spiritual intimacy with GOD. They both agreed that they wanted to rededicate their lives to Christ, and were led in prayer by the preacher.

Moreover, he told the couple how they needed to meditate on the Word of the LORD, reading their Bible daily, for as a Christian that is what feeds our spirit. He told them how scripture talks about the power of unity, how they need to fellowship with a body of believers – forsaking not the assembling of ourselves together as is the manner of some even more so as the great day of His coming approaches when all of the saints will be called away in a moment – in the twinkling of an eye – to meet Him in the air. Beyond all of this, Pastor Jackie and Sister Penny asked the couple if it'd be alright with them if they anointed them with oil, prayed over them, anointed the walls of rooms, door posts, and so forth, praying over their house and cleansing it from any unclean thing to which they gladly accepted.

Far from the melodrama of what Pastor Jackie had imagined, this was just a hurting people that wanted to be set free from the bounds of the enemy. After they prayed for her, the woman had cried and said that it felt like such a weight had been lifted off of her in so much that she felt lighter. There was a goodness of GOD that they'd left behind in that place. The works and darkness had been renounced, and GOD had welcomed these two wandering sheep back into the fold – which had left them open to being attacked by wolves.

As they made the drive home, the Nobles along with the host of Heaven rejoiced at what had happened there that night. There was so much goodness and grace that had been imparted upon them and flowed through their ministry ever since GOD delivered Larry during that school bus exorcism one week ago. It seemed clear to them in their minds that whatever The LORD was doing, it was continuing to propel upward like a rocket into space. In fact the only thing that troubled them was any tension, troublemaking, or hurt revolving around their pianist Sister Betty Sue Riley's deliverance.

Each night before bed, as well as on and off through the week, both Jackie and Penny would pray for her, just as they'd pray for all of their flock – howbeit, her even more so due to necessity. They slept well, each dreaming of bringing glory to the name of The LORD. Until the alarm that Penny had set for her husband woke him up. She herself had an internal sort of clock and always had. His waking was more attuned to the sound of her faithfully moving around in the kitchen to make him breakfast, the whistling of a coffee pot signaling that a fresh cup of his precious Maxwell House blend wasn't far behind.

Usually, on Saturdays the alarm wasn't set. This only happened on one Saturday each month. This was the fourth Saturday; the day that was the Reverend Jackie Noble's turn to go down to the local nursing home, preach, sing, pray for, and visit with the elderly. Some of the elderly ladies would say that he reminded them of a beau they used to have. Others would ask him didn't he live on the same street as them growing up. There would be a jolliness to this one, and a sadness to others. The more unfortunate ones would tell him how their children just left them there and never came to see them. He and the other ministries that came were by far the most enjoyable time for some.

They'd sing, and clap, and play music, preach a simple message, like one would to a children's class, about stories such as Daniel in the Lion's Den, Jonah in the Whale, Noah's Ark, and others that the group had grown up hearing about in church. LORD knew that every one of them would gladly be prayed for and every one of them – as we all do – needed all of the prayer that they could get. There Jackie and the other preachers would speak peaceable words of comfort over these overlooked, downcast people whom GOD loved, and they were happy to do so.

This day, just like any other, would begin with a hot cup of coffee. Penny and Jackie would delightfully verbally pick at one another. She'd thereafter smile and scrunch her nose. Like the prayerful ministerial excursion the night before when they aimed to face off against the demonic – Penny also accompanied her Jackie to the old folks home every fourth Saturday.

When they arrived, they walked down the hallway asking various old folks if they wanted to come and have church. Those who enthusiastically said "yes" were either

told where it'd be or for those who preferred, rolled down in wheelchairs. A few of the more ornery residents answered "no" with some indignancy, though a few of them otherwise enjoyed the weekly services and were wheeled in by staff a bit after the start.

Once in the dining room, which housed a piano, Jackie and Penny shook hands with the forming congregation of people. Prior to their arrival they had questioned one another whether they thought that Sister Betty would be there, as she usually was, to accompany the two of them on the old upright piano for the congregational singing, before ducking out before the sermon ended on her way to work. That would have been too routine, after all, thus the two of them waited a little longer than they otherwise would, hoping that she'd make it, only to find that she was not coming.

Pastor Jackie apologized for her absence to all of those attendees who were cognizant of it and then told them reassuringly how the Bible says that where two or three are gathered together in Christ's name, the power and presence of the Almighty will be also.

"We have a whole lot more than that here today. Did you know that with our faith – the faith like a child – that mountains can be moved and cast into the sea? We're serving a GOD who makes the impossible possible, the undoable doable, the unthinkable happen right before our eyes. The Bible says that 'eye has not seen nor ear heard, neither has it entered into the heart of man, the things that GOD has prepared for them that love Him!

"I wish that somebody would get excited in this place and praise the LORD. C'mon, y'all, sing this song and worship with us. Let's get loosened up and watch the Spirit of The LORD move here in this place," Jackie exclaimed in preacher-tones – hacking a bit here and there as he made such declarative statements of faith.

Then he began to play and sing as their opening song – If You're Happy and You Know It – going into the "clap your hands," "say amen," "stomp your feet," and – then on their fourth round – "do all three." Penny joined in with the singing and actively demonstrated and encouraged others to join in with the clapping, saying amen, those who could to stomp their feet, and all who were able to do all three.

After this, they went into a series of hymns that most people raised in church know. First was "Amazing Grace." Some of the old-timers raised their hands in worship, some sang along, and others eyes filled with tears during it. They also sang and played, "I'll Fly Away," "Meeting In the Air," and "Heaven's Jubilee." The word that Pastor Jackie brought that morning concerned the story of David and Goliath with the message being how there is nothing too big for GOD to do. When it all came to a close, Jackie asked individuals if they'd like prayer – going to one, then another, along with his wife. They'd dab their fingertips with the anointing oil from the small bottle that she carried with her in her purse and gently cry out to GOD on their behalf, speaking kindly words of comfort with a spirit of grace to them as they did it.

Whereas Jackie normally took Penny to the grocery store every Monday evening after the two of them had had supper – a time that Betty Sue Riley was rarely, if ever, working the checkout line – today they'd decided to make an additional trip to gather a few things with the distinct purpose of running into her and seeing that she was okay, whether she'd be back in

church with them the next Sunday, and that things would return to normal. GOD knew that if she didn't, their only recourse would be to have Eleanor Fitzgerald play in her stead. And while Eleanor could play the piano, she lacked the ability to play the Pentecostal notes and chords between the regular notes and chords, nor could she play by ear as Betty Sue could.

Eleanor could only read music and thereby played exactly as it was written. Moreover, if she did have the ability to transpose into a more appropriate key for the congregation or person singing, no one would ever know it, as it had never happened. As it has been well noted by very many people, the songs within hymnals tend to be written far higher than most people can comfortably sing them – thereby while the sheet music is meant to help the musician, it should be altered to accompany what suits the singer's – and moreover - the congregation's – vocal range the best. And knowing this only gave the Nobles one more reason to make the additional trip to the Cas Walker Store, where Betty Sue Riley worked a checkout line.

As with any day, people seemed excited to shop in this place. They had their Blue Band Coffee and other such things that folks came there to get. There was always a special sale on one thing or another. Therefore, loading up on some bargains and helping to make themselves look more sincere, Penny went down the aisles, adding one thing and then another to her cart as her husband-pastor helplessly followed. There she also saw acquaintances with whom she carried on conversations, asking about their mother, children, or friend of a neighbor's cousin that she was privy to. With Jackie beside her, he too would be pulled into nearly every conversation to an extent that it made it all too apparent to him that many of these people seemed to

know very much about the common ins and outs of his life due to previous conversations they'd had with his Penny.

And besides all of this, there was also the matter of him now being somewhat famous by way of the newspaper. Strangers would pull him aside and tell him about their walk with Christ or lack thereof and how they, too, felt they had witnessed manifestations of the demonic. Then, going into detail, they'd tend to want to know just what he thought about that. And while this saved him from talking about the most personal dealings of his day-to-day, it also kept him from being with his Penny as she journeyed off with the cart to GOD knows where. While this person or that more or less held him – passing the famed local preacher around as gents trade off a pretty girl at a dance whom they all wish to dance – he was pulled over here by this one and spun over there by that one, or so in his mind it seemed, anyway.

Every now and then an announcement would sound out, and people would seem to gravitate towards some new area where there was a limited sale – just like the blue-light specials at the local K-Mart. By gosh, if they could do it, then Cas Walker could do it too – he thought. It was quite possible that no man he'd ever known might be as brilliant in running a grocery chain as the eccentric, variety-show running, Knoxville-Tennesseean, elected official Cas Walker – who had thousands of stores stretching over different state lines all through the South.

He'd contributed heavily to the carrier of Dolly Parton, who first appeared on his show at 10 years old. The Everly Brothers were on in the 1950s. He regularly had guests like Jim Nabors and others – and though he was a man of great reputation on this day, to Jackie at

least, it seemed like people wanted to talk about him –
the Exorcist Preacher.

Breaking through all of this, his wife called out
from the end of the aisle, "Are you ready, dear? You
know that you've gotta prepare for your sermon
tomorrow. I've got everything that I need. C'mon, let's
move on out." And with that, she turned the buggy to
move on to the checkout counter. Seeing it, Jackie
could not help but hear her words repeat – I've got
everything I need. To which he thought – I bet; it looks
like you bought a good part of the store.

The cart was heaped high – high enough to keep
them in the checkout lane for a while. It'd take time to
ring all of those items up, and while this was going on,
Penny could talk to Betty Sue. Yessir, Penny Noble's mind
was set like a steel trap, swift and cunning, and yet she
had so much sweetness that she used to kneed it all
together like warm dough by way of her exquisite
bedside manner. You see, while some pastor's wives are
a noose around their neck, women like Penny Noble
were a help to their husbands. When Proverbs 31 was
written, it was written about this rare, industrious, prayerful
breed to which she belonged. While Penny bore no
children, she was like a mother to many, a sister to
others, and a friend.

Patiently they waited in the line, or that is when
Jackie finally broke through to catch up to her. To him, it
almost seemed like he could hear chatter asking
whether that man up there was the preacher who'd run
the devil out of Georgia, and others saying that they
knew he was 'cause they'd overheard conversations
about it in the store – but he paid them no mind. He was
a man on a mission. One of the sheep from his fold was

mere feet from him and he was now standing by his sweet Penny's side.

"So how much did you save me this time?" Jackie wisely asked – looking at the sizable sum of groceries that would doubtlessly hold them over for a while.

"Below that bag of peaches – next to the watermelon – are three jars of that coffee you like," she told him.

"Three?" he questioned.

"They were on sale," she answered.

"Why three?" he said, not that it wasn't favorable to know that he'd have a strong supply.

"Because that was the sale," she finally answered before they came to the counter where they'd have to unload their groceries.

As she was exceptionally busy at work it was only a little before this that Betty Sue had called over and seen them.

"Good Morning, Sister Penny. Good morning, Pastor. I sure didn't expect to see the two of you here today" she told them as they began to get the items to her and she began to ring them – thereafter sending each one on it's way to be bagged and placed in the afore cart – which was the cycle of how they'd load 'em up and move 'em out from store to car at the Cas Walker Grocery Store.

Some chatter went on thereafter and then Betty was told how they sure did miss her at the old folks home that morning as well as worship service on Wednesday night.

Responsively, Betty Sue went on with some excuses as to how life had been busy and all. You know, the sort of things that a person says when they're trying to avoid what really needs to be said, 'cause they just don't want to say it? And therein as this conversation furthered, despite all carefulness on Sister Penny's part, Betty Sue's voice began to crack as though she was about to cry. Frantically, she rushed through ringing out the groceries, but there were just so many. As they, talked she began to break down a bit further, with little being said or done. Finally, she called out to one of the front managers to take over and cover her while she took her break.

Penny then told Jackie to take care of their purchases and load the groceries into the car, as she would not be long. And with that, gracefully – like a swan swimming along a still, smooth pond – his wife wound and weaved amidst the people in the busy grocery store – coming alongside Betty Sue, placing her arm around her, and speaking soft sweet words of comfort as the two of them disappeared from view.

Thus the manager rang up his things, somewhat slowly and intrigued – and finally asked, wasn't he that preacher who cast out them devils in the newspaper? Jackie smiled politely and let out a sigh. Until he and Penny returned home, it was going to be a long day. Finally, making it back to the station wagon, he loaded it up, cracked the windows and turned on the air.

"One-Mississippi, two-Mississippi…" Jackie Noble sat there and counted for a while.

He'd reached somewhere between 200-300 Mississippi as far as his words went, though with the uneven rate of his counting, both in speeding up and slowing down, the count was arbitrary. Rather than listening to his beloved Hemphill's 8-Track – he did have others – Jackie turned on the radio to listen to the local gospel station which shortly thereafter cut out of one song that it was playing and into the Rev. Jimmy Swaggart singing the Dottie Rambo song, "Build My Mansion (Next Door To Jesus)." That song, as well as many of the songs she'd written, had done quite well that year. The Rambos had multiple songs out on the radio and were frequently in such heavy rotation that they were no stranger to the gospel music charts. He'd often seen such groups coming up as he attended all-night sings and so forth throughout the Georgia area, and likewise was fortunate enough to catch many of them during The National Quartet Convention's one-year-stay in Atlanta (circa 1960). Prior to that, it was primarily held in Memphis, Tennessee since the year of its founding in 1957. Its first move was its one-year stay in Birmingham, 1959 – then to Atlanta, 1960 – then back to Memphis, 1961-1971 – where it was acquired by J. D. Sumner (one of its founders). In this year of 1972, it moved to Nashville, Tennessee – where Jackie had heard that they intended to keep it, or for a while, anyway. Southern Gospel was a part of the South. It was GOD's music and it streamed across the country. Gloria Gaither was a preacher's kid from Michigan, and her husband Bill was a hoosier. While sin seemed to abound, at least on Jackie Noble's car radio, GOD's grace abounded more.

It was around about eighteen to twenty minutes from the time that Penny fluttered off to go and talk with Betty Sue – as the poor, distraught woman made haste to pull herself back from the public eye. Finally, after several songs had played through – she got in the car.

"Glad you could make it," Jackie jested with a smile.

"There was no rush, dear. It's not like we bought ice cream or anything," she somewhat gleefully told him, as the sausage patties and thick cut bacon rested somewhere behind them in a grocery bag.

As Pastor Jackie drove, he asked, or rather invited, his wife to tell him what had happened, merely by saying the word – "Well?"

From that point unto their way home, there into the house as he helped her unpack the groceries while she put them in their appropriate places – the places they'd always been, though it yet seemed a mystery to him – she continued to hash and rehash every detail of their conversation. The long and short of it was that she felt too embarrassed to return to church after everything that happened.

"You know how people are," Penny stated, though it was unclear whether it was an affirmation or question.

"What people?" Jackie said… or possibly just thought.

He wasn't quite sure.

Regardless, she went on to tell her story, which again prompted the line that he – the discerning pastor, the shepherd of their flock – knew how people were. Again, at this, he asked,

"What people? Gertrude Miller? Sister Trish? Who?"

His question came with no answer.

Since the whole account with Betty Sue Riley's demonic manifestation, Pastor Jackie had begun to study. From what he'd previously understood, a Christian couldn't even have a demon, and yet from what he had experienced, a question was raised as to whether this theology was on course with the actual doctrine taught in the Bible. Certainly, before the deluge of Noah we'd not heard of demonic possession – though it was a wicked and demonic time indeed. Mankind threatened to be wiped out as the abominable offspring of fallen angels and womankind walked the land as fierce giants. Being slain in the flood – their spirits were eternally damned to roam this earth. They would hunger and not be filled. They'd lust, but be empty. All of their indulgent desires would be with them and these now accursed formless beings, begotten of the fallen and sinful women, who were slain because of their horrendous evils – would be called – amidst other things – unclean spirits.

Far removed from the principalities, powers, and rulers of darkness, these low-level beings would only add to tormenting and corrupting mankind. And yet still, the spiritual realm is not like the pious physical. These beings cannot and do not go where they do not have the authority to go. Like Dracula, the door has to be opened. They have to have some kind of permission to come in. Certainly, there are Christians that struggle. While they're saved, they wrestle with sin, addiction, and the like. They

can be filled with the Holy Ghost with the evidence of speaking in tongues and still do and say things they ought not do and have need to repent over. Why would anyone think that demonic influence is any different?

The Bible even goes to lengths to teach that it is not. When someone carefully studies GOD's Word, the false doctrines of man crumble. Having relayed to him how his dear beloved sister – who should be rejoicing and free – struggled, Jackie agonized in asking himself what manner of church this was that he pastored where someone felt too rejected to come and join with them. Now there was a newfound determination within him. Tomorrow at church he was going to teach on the ministry of deliverance, the church's call to embrace it, and much of its historical failure to do so.

CHAPTER 04

An Introductory
Oration on Deliverance

It was Sunday, August 27th, 1972. The escalating whistle of the coffee pot in the Noble home began to sing the song of morning. Penny darted and dashed throughout the kitchen with the grace and ease of a professional chef and dancer combined. As always, she looked more ready than not, but such was her way. After a long day of studying before, Jackie did not feel so much tired as he did energized. Still, there was something of agitation and grief stirred up by the fact that Betty Sue Riley felt too awkward or ashamed to come to the church where she'd belonged for years.

Frankly, she felt like as much of an intricate part of it as the pastor did. The way she played those ivory keys was part of the flavor and tone of the place. While it was hopeful that none came merely for the music, nor to hear Pastor Jackie, but rather to feel the presence and power of GOD – her not being there and for such a reason as she had given was still a sad change to things.

"Good morning, Sunshine," Jackie playfully called as he entered the kitchen, thereafter planting a kiss on his wife's cheek.

"Well, would you look at you being all bright-eyed and bushy-tailed this morning? And there I was wondering if you were gonna get any sleep at all," she told him with something of a grin on her face.

"It's the anointing, dear," he retorted with a wink.

"I'll say," Penny conferred.

In the midst of this she didn't miss a beat: pouring coffee, cooking sausage and eggs. It was a juggling act that she was all too familiar with – and had attained mastery at doing.

On this Sunday, Pastor Jackie didn't only feel ready, but he had gotten ready, both in study and seeking the Holy Spirit to move mightily upon him. To put it mildly, at the beginning of this day, the man had some extra pep in his step. The loveliness of their morning continued, following them down to the church for the preservice tidying. As expected, all of the usuals were there – with the exception that this time, Brother Vincent and Sister Shirley arrived before Sister Young. As Sister Young walked in the door, Jackie poked fun at her, exclaiming to his sister in Christ how she was late. Of course, their poking at each other went both ways as she in turn asked him if he planned to preach over an hour and twenty minutes that morning.

Smiling, Jackie answered that if the Holy Ghost wanted him to, he would. Continuing to spar playfully, Sister Young asked him what if he did, and it wasn't by the Holy Ghost's leading. Jackie chuckled and told her that in that case, he'd owe everyone there an apology. They both laughed and continued the hurried cleaning before the Sunday school crowd arrived.

That morning, Tony Edwards taught about the value of praying in The Spirit – i.e. tongues; in a Heavenly language, as spoken of in scripture. His lessons, which really were more of sermons, weren't set by some book purchased through an organization or school, but whence ever he felt to speak from The LORD. Whereas a stirring word like this would generally turn into a full-blown Holy Ghost-filled shouting service with Sister Betty Sue Riley silently approaching the piano with such subtly that none seemed to notice and then bursting out into fiery Pentecostal licked on the piano, stacking notes upon notes, and playing soul-stirring music – on this day, the piano remained untouched until Sunday school was dismissed. Certainly, people did praise The LORD, get happy, and whatnot, but it was different without Sister Betty Sue there.

On cue, Sister Eleanor approached the piano and turned in the Red-Back Hymnal to page 99: "Faith of Our Fathers" – which is written in Eb and in 3/4 time, page 288: "Never Alone" – which is written in C in 6/8 time, and finally page 157: "Trust and Obey" – which is written in F and is also in 3/4 time. To Pastor Jackie, this is how it felt for someone not to go with the flow. Just when the service is going one way, the Holy Spirit is doing one thing, you'd knee jerk into the opposite way of things like Sister Eleanor just did. Nonetheless, the people's time to bless The LORD with their giving came and went, as did prayer, and then finally the time for him to deliver the morning's sermon began.

"For those of you who have your Bibles – and I hope that you do – please turn to the 15th chapter of Matthew," Pastor Jackie said.

Thereafter, as any preacher worth his salt, he said a few words for the value of saying them, but likely even more so to allow the congregants the time to turn to the passage of scripture that would be his key text instead of flying through it like a bat out of Hell while members frantically turned – losing sight of what he was saying in

their desperate struggle to catch up. Thereby, he continued.

"If we were a Catholic church, the focus point of the sermon would be taking the Holy Communion, the Eucharist, The LORD's Supper, to remember what He had done for us until the day that He comes again in clouds of Glory. It would be at this time in the service where a priest would deliver a shortened form of a sermon called a homily, and thereafter progress towards the Holy Communion.

Friends, we're gathered here together today because of who Jesus is, because of who He has called us to be, because of what He has called us to do. The church isn't just a hospital for the weak and sick. The church isn't just a training ground for war. The church isn't just a place to fellowship with friends and family. The Church is all of those things and so much more. If you came here today to hear me preach, or to hear Sister Eleanor play, or to hear Sister Martha sing, then you came for the wrong reason. You ought to have come to get something from GOD. You ought to strive to walk closer with Him and know more of Him.

The Bible says in Matthew 15, beginning at the twenty-first verse: 'Then Jesus went thence, and departed into the coasts of Tyre and Sidon. And, behold, a woman of Canaan came out of the same coasts, and cried unto him, saying, Have mercy on me, O Lord, thou Son of David; my daughter is grievously vexed with a devil. But he answered her not a word. And his disciples came and besought him, saying, Send her away;

for she crieth after us. But he answered and said, I am not sent but unto the lost sheep of the house of Israel. Then came she and worshipped him, saying, Lord, help me. But he answered and said, It is not meet to take the children's bread, and to cast it to dogs. And she said, Truth, Lord: yet the dogs eat of the crumbs which fall from their masters' table. Then Jesus answered and said unto her, O woman, great is thy faith: be it unto thee even as thou wilt. And her daughter was made whole from that very hour.'

Church, travel back with me, if you will, to this dramatic scene in the ministry of Jesus Christ. The very first miracle that Christ performed in the Gospel of Mark was the casting out of a devil from a congregant in a synagogue. Thereafter, the Bible tells me that Christ continued to go through the area to synagogues and cast out demons. Throughout the gospels, believers – who worshiped the one true GOD, who strived after holiness, who sought to keep the whole law, who sought to keep the sabbath, and who very likely lived more Christ-like lives than many so-called Christians today – were afflicted by the demonic. And then this happens. In His ministry, Christ directly focused on the Jewish people, but this gentile woman came to Him. She was a lost, pagan, sinner, but she had faith. Knowing that Jesus Christ had the power to heal her daughter, she pled for Him to do so – and Jesus told her that…" Pastor Jackie said pausing for dramatic emphasis before continuing.

"DELIVERANCE IS THE CHILDREN'S BREAD," he thereafter stated emphatically.

The congregation of Souls Harbor Holiness Church was quiet. Perhaps there may have been a yes or an amen out of politeness, but was it merely for show? Had his message even thus far hit the mark? Certainly, the man-made doctrines of religion had taught such fallacies as a true Christian couldn't be touched by the Devil, and yet scripture made it so plainly apparent that we could be attacked, we could be suppressed, we could engage in a struggle, we could be tempted. And yet there are far too many Biblical accounts to cite and list – in such an extreme that these matters should be overwhelmingly self-evident. Their call was one of persistence and faithfulness.

Did these people really grasp the word of GOD on these matters? His heart was so broken for his dear sister Betty Sue, whom GOD had set free, only to feel as though she were a rose plucked up and trampled on the ground. Thereby, with firmness, he held his Bible high up in the air over his head and again yelled in thunder tones, "DELIVERANCE IS THE CHILDREN'S BREAD! Deliverance isn't salvation, but it is a benefit of being in the presence of Jesus Chirst. The Pharisees asked what sort of new doctrine this was that Jesus cast out demons. You see, everything that he taught had been taught before. He brought truth and expounded on truth, but Christ's ministry did not merely come with the brilliance of thought and vernacular. The Gospel of Christ came with power and authority.

"Scripture tells us that this is the finger of GOD – casting out demons. It tells us that the sign that GOD's Kingdom is here on Earth is that demons are being cast out. The church isn't supposed to date Jesus. The church isn't supposed to be buddies with Jesus. The Church is called to be His perfect bride. Outside of only a few examples of

this woman and the instance of the man living in the tombs – who was possessed with a legion of demons – we find again and again that He was bringing deliverance to people within The Church," Pastor Jackie continued.

And as his sermon had begun, so did it carry on, never once straying from course. Every word was so intentional. It was all handed to them in such a way that it seemed so easy that a child might understand it. He talked about the boy afflicted by a deaf and mute spirit – the same who convulsively frothed at the mouth and cast the boy into fire and water trying to kill him. He spoke of how Christ taught that once a demon was cast out of a person, they'd go through the dead, dry, desolate places, seeking rest but finding none, and thereby would hunger to return to that person from whom they were cast out. It was highly evident that if this person was a sinner and would remain a sinner, they'd suffer a far worse thing than they had before – making it better if the devil within them had never been cast out in the first place.

Fully being aware of this, it says much about the amassment of people from whom Christ exorcized devils. The man from the tombs became an evangelist of Christ in the land of the Gadarenes. Certainly, the woman, too, must have had an encounter with GOD, both literally and metaphorically on the same level as Naaman the leper (2 Kings 5) or the widow woman whose GOD supernaturally gave an increase of oil throughout the entirety of the famine that plagued the land for aiding His servant – the prophet Elijah (2 Kings 4). Beyond these conversions, the demoniacs were all Jews. Mary Magdalene had seven devils cast out of her. She was one of the few who was there at the cross amidst the

other women, with the Apostle John being the only one of the twelve disciples there.

Point by point, his message came, and thereon Pastor Jackie proceeded into naming off other scriptures where the furtherance of what was ordained in the 16th chapter of Mark would come forth. He read:

> "'For in the case of many who had unclean spirits, they were coming out of them shouting with a loud voice; and many who had been paralyzed and lame were healed. – ACTS 8:7'"

Pastor Jackie likewise noted how the exorcisms were happening in such abundance – along with other signs, miracles, and healing – that it captured the attention of the world, both those who looked favorably on this doctrine come – seen as a fulfillment of the Messianic Covenant by those within it – known as THE WAY, for Jesus Christ – the second person in the GODHEAD – is the only way to the Father in Heaven.

Due to this, many mystics, heretics, and such sought to invoke the power of the name of Jesus Christ – GOD incarnate – of whom there is none higher in Heaven, on Earth, or below the Earth. This was told in the Acts of the Apostles with the account of a vagabond Jew named Sceva and his seven sons. They came to a demoniac and adjured those devils to come out in the name of Jesus Christ whom Paul preaches. To this, the devils replied "Jesus we know and Paul we know, but we don't know you." Upon saying this, they lept out of the man who they had possessed and entered into these brash, unsaved, degenerate, mystic fools, causing them to tear off their clothes and thrash around violently in such a way that scripture describes the terrifying scene as one where they all left that place naked and wounded, and the fear of The LORD came upon all who knew of it.

Of course the demons' knowledge of who Jesus Christ was– GOD, in coming down as man – is extraordinarily evident in scripture, for they attested to it in the Gospels. Moreover, because of his walk with Christ, the Apostle Paul was called out and harassed by a demon spirit of divination who inhabited a young slave girl, from whence he expelled her in ACTS 16:16-18.

If ever a perfect introductory sermon had been preached or taught touching the realization that Christians could be subject to demonization, this might have been it, for aside from these points, Pastor Noble spoke of holiness and how we're not to give place to the devil. He brushed over a thing here and then explained there as to how one can have soul ties, be subject to generational curses, and do other things to give the demonic permission to enter into ourselves.

Moreover, he touched on the fact that while GOD is a triune being – comprised of GOD the Father, GOD the Son, and GOD the Holy Ghost – we, too, are triune beings – comprised of our body, spirit, and soul. And while the demonic could not separate us from the love of GOD, nor directly impact our salvation, they could find access to that multi-chambered part of ourselves, which is our spirit. He pointed out that this is why GOD wants complete access to every part of our lives. In those rooms where we seek to keep Him out, devils might slip in and hide in the shadows.

Devils are certainly good at hiding. They can hide in the light. For all of some of those people's lives who sat there in the synagogues, prayed, and worshiped, those demons had never once slithered like snakes out of their

holes, yet when Christ came, He exposed and expelled them. So devils can hide even in the light, so long as there is a little darkness in it that leaves them room to do so.

He ended his message asking that the congregation would still remember Sister Betty Sue.

Like so many sermons preached by so many preachers, the usual congregants would shake his hand and tell him how they enjoyed it. They'd say that it was good preaching, how they enjoyed that good word, and all of the normal church "at-a-boys" that church people say to a minister. Still, he wondered if what he had said had done any good at all. Did his words fall on deaf ears? Jackie Noble's shepherd's heart grieved deeply within him. He asked himself inwardly whether there was a goat among his fold. Was there a tear among the wheat? Were some of the people confused, or perhaps Betty Sue was just mistaken about the whole thing?

After the morning service ended, Pastor Jackie, along with several others, went to the Ponderosa – their local buffet –where they ate, drank, and merrily conversed as though nothing was going on. It was just like one of their very own hadn't fallen by the way, and yet it seemed that she had, and perchance he and his wife alone mourned her. While the people joked and carried on, this pastor wore a smile – as we all do from time to time when we don't feel like smiling at all. He could only think of how deeply it hurt him to see someone take a step back when by all accounts they should be moving forward.

With all of this said, it bears mentioning that the long-time church regulars weren't the only ones in attendance that Sunday. Those same young people –

who'd witnessed the school bus exorcism, the creekside baptismal procession, and a demon spirit being cast out of Betty Sue Riley right in the middle of Sunday Morning Worship – had been attending faithfully. They, too, were there with them at the Ponderosa. They were a bright point to Jackie. Certainly, these youths weren't the problem but the solution. They had that fresh kind of zeal and energy that a new convert tends to have. They'd not fallen victim to piety, being gospel-hardened, or any such thing. Their only disadvantage was that they were yet novices in the faith. However, any Christian, at any time, anywhere has been in their same shoes. They merely need to apply themselves in the Word of GOD, and be faithful, steadfast, and unmovable in their faith to see The LORD do great things through them.

As he thought about the two of them at the table, sitting somewhat quietly and somewhat enamored by him – the Holy Ghost-filled, tongue-talking, devil-slaying, glory-hallelujah-shoutin' preacher man – a warmth filled his heart, and thus he began to speak with the two of them in such a way that it was as though no one else at all was there in the room. Their names were Daphne Blake and Josie McCoy. While Pastor Jackie didn't own a television or have anything to do with cartoons – with the mild exclusion of reading Beetle Bailey or one of the other comic-strips in the funny pages – they informed him that each of their names were the exact names of cartoon characters belonging to different series. As he was brought to understand through their conversation, the character Daphne Blake – who shared the name with one of these girls – was the most glamorous member of a group of detectives, known as Mystery Inc., on a CBS Television show titled after a pothead youth's dog, Scooby Doo, who accompanies them. The cartoon character was a redhead and wore a purple and green outfit. Meanwhile, the other girl, whose name was Josie

McCoy, had a cartoon alter-ego that was also a fiery red-headed lead singer and the guitarist of an all-girl pop-rock band.

Conversely, it was strange that both of the cartoon characters were redheads, as it is not that common of a thing. When hearing that the one girl's character which bore her name played the guitar – he raised an eyebrow and asked her if she had ever wanted to learn – adding how if she did, he could teach her a few chords. It was all but a moot point, something of amusement to many, as most people tended to watch television and thereby knew who these people were. Still, he took it all in politely. His interest was more in these girls as people, their spiritual wellness and walk with Christ, and the transformative change that He could bring about in them. And it was because he genuinely cared that he took an interest in them and what they had to say.

He wanted for the girls to feel open and comfortable talking with him. Jackie asked them about school, whether they liked it or not, asked them about their lives, sports, whether either of them had a boyfriend, and such things. Moreover, as these were both females, Penny chimed in, interrelating with them quite a bit more than her kindhearted husband could. Certainly, there was some talk and conversation with the others at the table, all of whom he loved so very much, but these were the baby Christians. They were the ones who needed to be trained and nurtured. Within church, anyway, they were uncorrupted. Just like a baby rattlesnake's venom is more potent than an adult rattlesnake, Jackie thought how these girls might good and well add fresh fire to the altar of The LORD, bringing glory to His name.

After all of this came the Noble's Sunday afternoon nap. While neither of them were old, this did seem like a good time to re-energize between the two services. Jackie Noble's evening sermon followed his morning sermon perfectly. It took their parishioners to the same point in time when Jesus Christ had begun His earthly ministry – this time in Luke 4. Like in Mark 1 and Matthew 4, in this chapter, He'd just left the wilderness, having been tempted by Satan. His key text was LUKE 4:16-21, which reads:

> "And he came to Nazareth, where he had been brought up: and, as his custom was, he went into the synagogue on the sabbath day, and stood up for to read. And there was delivered unto him the book of the prophet Esaias. And when he had opened the book, he found the place where it was written, 'The Spirit of the Lord is upon me, because he hath anointed me to preach the gospel to the poor; he hath sent me to heal the brokenhearted, to preach deliverance to the captives, and recovering of sight to the blind, to set at liberty them that are bruised, To preach the acceptable year of the Lord.' And he closed the book, and he gave it again to the minister, and sat down. And the eyes of all them that were in the synagogue were fastened on him. And he began to say unto them, This day is this scripture fulfilled in your ears."

Therein, Jackie began to talk about all that had happened surrounding this text. The people there who knew Him as a child also knew His earthly family, Mary and Joseph. They thought Him to be the bastard son of Mary, not knowing that he was conceived of the Holy Spirit as He overshadowed Mary and supernaturally placed GOD inside of her. They knew his half-brother,

James (the same writer of the Epistle of James – found within the canonized New Testament), a Nazarite and martyr for Christ. Also, the head over the church at Jerusalem. Likewise, there were his brothers Joseph, Judas (author of the New Testament book of Jude), and Simon, as well as His half-sisters, whom Mary and Joseph bore.

Pastor Jackie thereby made the point that it was because of their unbelief that these people could not experience the fulfillment of what Christ had read before them. Thereafter, leaving and going to a synagogue in Capernaum, a city of Galilee, he cast a demon out of a parishioner in the middle of their Shabbat Service, and thereafter went all throughout that region doing the same. Again, Pastor Jackie emphasized the words that Christ had spoken – and most specifically in regard to this:

"To preach deliverance to the captives."

And with that, he posed the question, asking them, "What sort of person can be afflicted with an unclean spirit?" Of course, this question had already thoroughly been answered earlier that morning – howbeit, some people fail to grasp hold of even the most evident truths the first time. Thereby, he repeated it. One thing led to another, which took him up and down the trail where Christ told the gentile woman, who pled for her demonized little girl, that deliverance is the children's bread. Thereby, when we see Jesus Christ exclaiming that He was there to bring deliverance to the captives, we are given an outlying spiritual context of what manner of captivity He was speaking of.

After preaching for thirty-five minutes, Pastor Jackie told the audience that he believed that GOD was still the great deliverer, that GOD was still the great physician, and that GOD had not changed one iota since the very beginning of time. Several people prayed one for another. In all rights it was a wonderful service, yet Jackie wondered if anything had really changed. Certainly, he posed just as much of a threat to the demonic as when those two devils had manifested themselves before in his presence. Certainly, in every instance, GOD was faithful and the power of the Holy Spirit working within and from without him, and yet there were no further manifestations.

As it often does, silence creates room for contemplation. He wondered about his wayward sheep, Betty Sue. Her absence grieved him. Moreover, he saw ghosts as it is today in the congregation. Was this person or that person causing division? Crying out to The LORD, he pled for GOD to show him something. This ranting, vocal driving, and lamentation continued on well into the night after he and his wife had gotten home. Finally, as if from divine inspiration, Penny suggested that perhaps a demonic hold is like an addict or a child. They only begin to fight and resist when they're being deprived of that thing that they're on some level bound to.

It all seemed so simple and yet brilliant. With any sort of addiction or bad habits, we don't merely stop doing them, but we replace those bad things with better things. We leave one master who seeks to drive us into the ground for one who loves us. We put off a heavy yoke, and take on the yoke that Christ gives us – of which He said is light and easy. This filled him with a sort of conjuring articulation from whence he'd continue this Sunday's sermons into their Wednesday night. Shortly

before they went to bed – at an hour that was far later in the night than when they normally retired to their rest – Jackie approached his wife with his eyes ablaze with inspiration, and thus he read:

> "'From whence come wars and fightings among you? come they not hence, even of your lusts that war in your members? Ye lust, and have not: ye kill, and desire to have, and cannot obtain: ye fight and war, yet ye have not, because ye ask not. Ye ask, and receive not, because ye ask amiss, that ye may consume it upon your lusts. Ye adulterers and adulteresses, know ye not that the friendship of the world is enmity with God? whosoever therefore will be a friend of the world is the enemy of God. Do ye think that the scripture saith in vain, The spirit that dwelleth in us lusteth to envy? But he giveth more grace. Wherefore he saith, God resisteth the proud, but giveth grace unto the humble. Submit yourselves therefore to God. Resist the devil, and he will flee from you. Draw nigh to God, and he will draw nigh to you. Cleanse your hands, ye sinners; and purify your hearts, ye double minded. Be afflicted, and mourn, and weep: let your laughter be turned to mourning, and your joy to heaviness. Humble yourselves in the sight of the Lord, and he shall lift you up."
>
> – JAMES 4:1-10

Then he looked deep into Penny's eyes with a saddened, woeful expression. He sighed a slow, deep sigh as if deflated and ever so deeply grieved. Then the weary pastor asked her in all sincerity how it was that the church thought that they could ever lead the world to repent when it would not repent itself.

The two of them faithfully prayed, renouncing and denouncing every vile affection, ill thought, or evil that they might have even allowed to enter into their lives, their ministry, or their marriage. They defied the enemy and called out to the LORD how they surrendered everything that they stewarded and every part of themselves – even the most secret places, unto the LORD – knowing fully that the reason the devils don't fear the so-called church today in the way that they did in the New Testament is because today's church has more in common with the demonic than it does with GOD.

CHAPTER 05

At the Doorstep of Deliverance

In a manner of speaking, Jackie Noble awoke on Monday, August 28th, 1972, just like any other day. His morning coffee, breakfast with Penny, and even the early morning procedures at J.C. Penny went as to be expected. The thing that would be different would come hours later; for there on that day, in what seemed like out of the blue, Pastor Jackie's beloved friend and the man whom he thought of as his pastor, The Reverend Doctor Byron Phillips – whom he'd served under as the youth pastor at the sizable New Life Fellowship Church in West Point, Georgia – had come to visit him there at the store.

Driving all that way just to see him, have a conversation, and purchase a new pair of dress shoes, Dr. Phillips and Jackie smiled and carried on like the best of friends. Things were going well at New Life Fellowship. The church's attendance had grown, as had the expanse of their community outreach and giving to World Missions. Dr. Phillips told Jackie all of these things and then informed him that he'd heard from the Clark's about a school-bus exorcism that he'd performed on a young drug addict in a dilapidated school bus that was sitting derelict somewhere in the backwoods of their great state of Georgia. And while all of this was a surprise visit, Dr. Phillips eventually came around to telling Pastor Jackie that he'd not just traveled all of that way to see him and chew the fat. He'd come to talk to him about the upcoming camp meeting which was being held in Atlanta on Monday, September 18th, through Friday, September 22nd.

This was an event that Jackie and Penny had been looking forward to. They and other people in their church were planning on car pooling there, sharing some hotel rooms, and making a sort of Gospel vacation of it. In fact, people would be attending from all throughout the country and around the world. There, different ministers within their denomination would be delivering powerful words from GOD. There would be music, prayer, and thanksgiving. Together, they'd fellowship one with another. This annual camp meeting was always a joy to Jackie and so many others. For the longest time, he'd been a part of it, and every year he'd make plans to return again. Howbeit, this year was a bit different…

While the speakers in this were usually the folks that were regarded as "a somebody" – such as an elected official within their denomination here, someone's cousin, brother, dad, or son there – they'd be bound to be anyone but Jackie Noble, and yet because of Dr. Phillip's confidence in his former youth pastor, he informed Jack that the man scheduled to speak at their Friday morning service was in the hospital. Dr. Phillips had suggested that the committee let some new blood in it, and everyone had agreed that Pastor Jackie Noble ought to be approached about being their Friday-morning keynote speaker during camp meeting on that September 22nd.

"Wow. I really don't know what to say," Jackie told him.

"Say, 'yes,'" Dr. Phillips encouragingly replied. The two of them carried on with one another, and Jackie Noble's date with destiny was set.

Now, very often in years past, some families would come into the convention a bit late – say Tuesday or Wednesday – missing the opening services. Others would leave early, opting not to stay on Friday. It would always begin on a Monday evening. Tuesday morning was their dreaded organizational business meeting that dealt with doctrine, bylaws, amendments, and elections for church offices, including the committee that determines who would be speaking the next year: a committee that Dr. Byron Phillips fortuitously sat on at this given time. It was because of this that they'd always try to begin the conference by having their General Overseer preach on Monday night and some big headline speaker finish it off on Friday night. While the morning services paled in comparison to the attendance that the evening services held, their audience was still sizable and they were always spirit filled.

From an evangelistic and even electoral standpoint, speaking at their annual Camp Meeting in any regard was a way for someone to be known. And while this was not Jackie Noble's life endeavor, it certainly meant something to anyone to feel that they were genuinely valued. He had accepted the offer; he planned to prepare for this happy occasion, which was a mere three weeks away. When he arrived home, Jackie was beaming, and Penny saw it all over him. She told him cheekily that he looked so aglow that she wondered if he "might oughta veil his face like Moses" – after being a witness to the weight of the glory of The LORD. There in the kitchen the two of them carried on for a bit – as lovebirds do – and then he told her the good news.

Frankly, in a way, it was a wonder that he'd waited that long instead of calling her straight from work, but it had been an eventful day and the hours rolled by like minutes. While he carried on with each customer with a liveliness and certain sort of spunk to him, he had a new joyous happy thought – in regards to the excitement of preaching for his first time ever in front of such a large and prestigious assembly. There were so many preachers that could have been selected to fill in the space, and yet the board agreed to choose him. It was a high honor which he did not intend, by any means, to take for granted. And while this invitation was a grand and glorious feeling, at the present, Pastor Jackie still knew that he had to devote time to the preparation of his Wednesday-night sermon.

And so it came. Souls Harbor Church began its Wednesday-night service at the usual 6:30 p.m. Eastern Standard Time on August 30th, 1972. It had just been two Sundays ago when their Sister Betty Sue had been delivered from the hold of the demonic through the power of the Holy Ghost and authority of Jesus Christ in GOD the Father. Two days before the school-bus exorcism, yet still neither of these who GOD had set free had been among their church attendance since these things. The only new people attributed to any of this were the teenage girls, Daphne and Josie, who up until this point had never before come on a Wednesday night. This evening would be the first – for Josie, anyway. Faithfully, she'd ridden her bicycle there. Upon being asked about her friend, she told Sister Penny that Daphne had homework but that she had determined to go to their Wednesday-night worship service instead, see what it was all about, and copy off of someone early the next morning in class before turning in the finished assignments. It was ironic, as this service – like two

Sunday evenings before – would be a night to remember.

While there were certainly many people in the congregation who'd been healed of one thing or another through the power of prayer and grace of GOD, only one saved person had ever had a devil cast out of them there, and while Jackie became more and more aware that a born-again Christian could have an evil spirit dwelling in them – just like one could have vices, hang ups, addictions, or bad habits and still be saved – he knew that, like in the day of Jesus Christ, there were many within the church that wouldn't receive the truth about anything that they didn't want to, even when it was laid out before them in terms that even an unlearned child could understand.

Despite Sister Eleanor's by-the-book-only style of piano playing – which was often in the wrong key for Martha to sing – they had church that night. The people began to get into it. It wasn't so much anything that Jackie was saying but what GOD was doing. Yet, still, what he was saying had some effect.

"Submit yourself to GOD. Resist the devil and he will flee" he'd cry.

And yet he'd not just say empty words but expound on this point. Jackie spoke of the things that he and Penny had done without, for the sincere purpose of pursuing after the holiness of GOD. He talked about how they didn't wear wedding bands, nor did he wear a tie pin. He talked about how neither one of them even owned a short-sleeved shirt.

"There are some people who like to go to the beach for vacation. Why, I know that when Jesus Christ cast a legion of devils into a heard of pigs, the first thing that those demonized pigs did was put on some copper tone and went to the beach! But, Honey, I'm here to tell you just like Joshua told the people – 'As for me and my house we will serve The LORD!' I'm not ashamed of the gospel of Jesus Christ. Church, we're called to be upright and holy. It's time that the church fell on their faces with the fear and admonition of GOD and repented. I know that there are some who might call this legalism, but I'd rather be a legalist than illegal," he declared, all while the saints shouted up to the heavens.

It was during this time when two or three people went to shouting around the church. Another stood and began speaking with an unknown tongue as the Holy Spirit gave them utterance. Then someone – under the power of the Holy Ghost – interpreted it.

"'Thus saith The LORD, if my people, which are called by my name, shall humble themselves, and pray, and seek my face, and turn from their wicked ways; then will I hear from heaven, and will forgive their sin, and will heal their land. I've called you to be holy, church. Keep your wicks trimmed and burning. This is the word of The LORD,'" the translator said over the hushed crowd, which kept quiet during this moment, out of reverence (which was customary).'"

Then the service continued. Pastor Jackie said a little more of the walk that he, his wife, and so many other blessed saints walked for The LORD. These were people who didn't dance like the world danced. They didn't listen to secular music or go to public beaches or public pools, as that was reviled as what the church called mixed-bathing – which just sounds dirty. If they wanted to take a dip in the creek, Jackie would go down there with his shirt and belt on, roll up his pants cuffs a few times, bringing them the the middle of his calf, so they didn't flap around, keep his shirt cuffs buttoned, while still being tucked in and his belt still on. Penny, too, would be fully dressed, as she never wanted to be seen as immodest. She'd put a diaper pin in her skirt to keep it from flying up over her knees. This was the holiness way after all. And while it seemed that he could hardly say it anymore, Pastor Jackie kept on saying that we're meant to make our bodies a living sacrifice, holy, and acceptable before GOD, which is our reasonable service. Also, we are called to be holy – for He is holy.

The preaching just kept getting hotter and hotter. People continued shouting, dancing in the Spirit, running, and falling out on the floor while others were renouncing and denouncing their sins. There was one person at the altar on this side and two more at the other, with a person or two praying with each of them. Beneath the sound of Preacher Jackie's voice, you could hear one of those brothers, Johnny Lay, telling the fellow in the altar, who was shaking all over and crying, to hold on. Meanwhile the other brother, Rev. Todd Driscoll, who had ahold of the same man from his other side, was telling him to let go. A sister, Juanita Mullins, who was praying with another lady, was assuring her that Jesus didn't work off of a pie chart but He had an endless supply – and would surely meet her need.

"Go on and praise him, Saints. Praise the LORD. Praise the Most High," Jackie exclaimed as he took a brief break to take a drink of water from a cup made ready for him on one of the shelves inside the podium.

It was at this time that a man from out of their congregation came forward, directing his steps toward Pastor Jackie. He moved in close like he had something to say that he didn't want everyone to hear. Discerning this, Pastor Jackie approached him and asked what it was, and leaned in so as to listen closely to what his brother in Christ had to say.

"Preacher, I don't believe a Christian can have a demon. I just want you to pray that GOD would help me and what I'm going through," the man said.

Trying to oblige him, Jackie prayed what began as a somewhat eloquent prayer, asking that GOD touch his dear brother and so on and so forth, and then as he felt to led of The Spirit to do, he spoke the words,

"And in the Name of Jesus Christ I come against this spirit of death that seeks to take hold of my brother. You have no right here – let him go in Jesus name!"

It was at these words that something happened. That man who had walked up so normally was instantaneously knocked backward about ten to twelve feet and thrown out on the floor by a supernatural power. With everything else that was going on, not everyone's eyes were specifically on this occurrence as it had happened so far. Two of the men in their church

went over to help him up, when a shrill and angry voice cried out of this man that was not his own.

"He is mine, Man of GOD. I am on assignment. Let me be. This man belongs to me," it called out through him, as he had now sat up and began to stagger and wriggle his way up to a squat.

"I defy you, devil in the name of the LORD, GOD of Israel. Come out in Jesus name, and go back to Hell where you came from!" Jackie authoritatively commanded.

While this total encounter might have gone on for around five to ten minutes, it captivated, startled, and mesmerized those who were watching. Some joined their pastor in prayer. Others just watched as though it was some astounding thing going on at a carnival or something. At any rate, that thing left him.

Covered in sweat and tears, the delivered man put Jackie in the biggest bear hug and thanked him emphatically.

"God bless you, Preacher. God bless you," he wept.

Penny and Jackie were so very grateful for another soul set free from the bondage of the enemy. A few people talked about how that was really something. There was chatter about how they'd all really had church that night, yet unfortunately, it was not the opinion of them all. For a brief time, any descension was quiet. Then on the night of Friday, September 1st, 1972, the Nobles' phone rang.

The man on the other line was Jerry Walls. He was calling Pastor Jackie because of concerns that he had with deliverance messages being preached and the purported casting out of demons from saved people. He told him that he just didn't believe in all of that and that the next Sunday would be he and his family's last. Each word during this difficult conversation tore Jackie's heart all to pieces. He tried explaining to him and reasoning with him, but just as the religious Pharisees asked Jesus Christ to do a miracle for them – who had previously done so many miracles that all of the books in the world could not contain them – nothing he could say or do seemed to change Jerry's view of things, and they'd been together for years. Jerry and his family would often say how real their pastor and his wife were. They'd talk about how much confidence they had in him, and now they were leaving.

Jerry Walls had first come to Souls Harbor Holiness Church just a few weeks after Jackie and Penny were stationed there. At that time, he was really sick and within a month he was in the emergency room. Jackie Noble dropped everything to go down there and be with him. Jerry had a brain bleed, and while he was conscious, he was near death. Pastor Jackie quoted Ezekiel 16:6 over him, saying:

> "'And when I passed by thee, and saw thee polluted in thine own blood, I said unto thee when thou wast in thy blood, Live; yea, I said unto thee when thou wast in thy blood, Live.'"

Thereafter, he looked at brother Jerry straight in the eye and asked whether he felt GOD heal him right then and there. Being on meds and hooked to those machines, Jerry wasn't really in a place to say much, but he just knew that GOD had healed him. Later, the doctors confirmed that despite their lack of knowledge as to how he'd become well from a medical standpoint, the fact was that Jerry's condition had completely reversed. Instead of being at death's door, Jerry Walls was alive and well.

As he explained to Jackie that he was walking out on him and Souls Harbor Church, that occasion as well as all of the other times when he grieved and rejoiced alongside the Walls family replayed in the pastor's mind. This all was so difficult. First Betty Sue Riley had left, and now the Walls – a family of four.

After he got off of the phone, Pastor Noble, having a shepherd's heart, began to weep. Penny held him and prayed with her dear husband, assuring him that if they weren't on the right track, the Devil wouldn't be fighting them so hard. And so it was well into the night.

As all of this was ending and he was readying himself for bed, Penny opened her hope chest that she was given so many years ago. It was in there where she kept her special night gown. Despite her genuine modesty, it was sleeveless, long, ivory, smooth, and sleek to the touch. If she would ever have to get the door while wearing it, if there was a fire, or so forth, the Noble's had several house coats – which is to say, more than the two of them needed. Kindly and lovingly, she nestled up to her husband, coursing her hands up and down his arms, back, chest, and stomach.

"I'm so thankful that The LORD blessed us with one another," she told him.

And turning the lights out, the two of them found comfort in one another's embrace.

Jackie loved his Penny like Elkanah loved Hannah in scripture. Though she couldn't conceive a child, that was not to say that they didn't find intimate comfort with one another in the privacy of their bedroom. Saturday came and went. On the next Sunday morning – September 3rd, 1972 – Josie and Daphne would have a few more people with them at church, some of whom were their family members and others who were friends. To hear a few of them talk, they'd heard of the dramatic displays of GOD's power enacted through this country preacher, shoe salesman, and perhaps most appropriately: faithful servant of The LORD, the Reverend Jackie Noble. Sunday school would come and go, as would the song service – and while he tried his best to worship The LORD, and in fact did, all of this leaving business regarding Betty Sue Riley – and now Jerry Walls, his wife, and their two children – were likened to a sickness in the pit of his stomach.

Jackie's morning message came from the sixth chapter of the Gospel of John. There were several points in Jesus' earthly ministry when the crowd that followed him would become sizable. Seemingly, on every occasion that this happened, Jesus would say something that would as much as run off any of them who weren't His true followers, much to the heartbreak that it caused him. Jackie expounded how so many people attend church but lack a truly intimate walk with GOD. He then asked the people how often they spent time with The LORD during their day as opposed to other things? He interjected how while we know to tithe 10% of our money, should we not honor GOD with at least 10% of our time? After all, we choose the things that we love. Whether it be a concert, a dance, a ball game, a book, or television show, people put those things first in their lives that they value.

From thence he read the sixth chapter of John, where Jesus spoke to the people that if they do not eat His flesh and drink his blood – speaking of Holy communion – they're not worthy of Him. One after another, young and old who professed to be followers of The LORD – the masses abandoned Him. Rather notably this culminated in John 6:66, which reads:

> "From that time many of his disciples went back, and walked no more with him."

Specifically, the numbering of that verse – though later added for reference, seemed oddly indicative of something and worth mentioning. In scripture, the number six is the number of man. It was on the sixth day that GOD created man. When the Bible calls the Mark of the Beast six hundred and three-score and six (i.e. 666) – it is essentially indicative of a man saying: me, me, me. To this, Jackie thereby added that sometimes the decisions that we make don't come off as black and white as being between choosing Jesus or the Devil. Sometimes it's more of a choice between Jesus or you, but then that is all like discernment. As has been said, discernment isn't the difference in knowing right from wrong. Discernment is the difference in knowing right from almost right.

Finishing the sixth chapter of John, Pastor Jackie Noble then read verses 67-71, which say:

> "'Then said Jesus unto the twelve, Will ye also go away? Then Simon Peter answered him, Lord, to whom shall we go? thou hast the words of eternal life. And we believe and are sure that thou art that Christ, the Son of the living God. Jesus answered them, Have not I chosen you twelve, and one of you is a devil? He spake of

Judas Iscariot the son of Simon: for he it was that should betray him, being one of the twelve.'"

And thus even after this day that they read of in scripture, Christ was yet to be betrayed. And Pastor Jackie Noble, who read it, had far more things to suffer for the account of Christ as Betty Sue Riley and the Walls family were far from the only ones who'd leave him before this year transcended into the next.

Words could not express the sadness that their leaving brought him. People say how the church is like their family, and yet their families do far more to offend them than the church, yet they keep them, and push back the eternal. Still, he wore a smile, thankful for what he had been given despite Satan carrying those that he loved away.

CHAPTER 16

Unholy Convocation

In ministry, sometimes it seems that a person has to be like Nehemiah, who – under a strain from the enemy's attacks – is forced at a certain point to work with a tool in one hand and a weapon in the other, so to guard himself, that GOD's good work may proceed. Seemingly to him, this is the place where Jackie was in his mind's eye. He was building up the Kingdom of GOD. Would the enemy, too, hire false prophets against him to assault what Souls Harbor Holiness Church was doing with their words? – he wondered. Like many church things, even within an organization, this was all such a close-knit and internalized kind of thing. Jackie had more than enough to be worked up over with his being asked to speak at the prestigious camp meeting, to where his congregants and other attendees from hundreds of other holiness churches embarked annually.

A place of relief was in the minister Todd Driscoll, who attended his church. Todd was a lay preacher, getting up to speak ever so often within their particular church and, on occasion, evangelizing in the not-too-far-off area. He even worked with a small after-school Bible program as the monitoring adult, though that had failed to bring in any new youth to their church. To the contrary, the thing that was bringing young people in was the same thing that had driven others out – the

supernatural deliverance of Almighty GOD. This all seemed so odd. They weren't a some dead, dried-up church who'd never felt a move of The Spirit, sending people to shouting praises to The LORD, lifting up holy hands without wrath or doubting, nor were they like the cessationist Baptist Church, who might ask someone to leave for speaking in tongues as the Holy Spirit genuinely gave them utterance. These were Pentecostals. They believed in healing. They believed in the continuance of the gifts of The Spirit. To put it plainly: they believed the Bible, or so they said.

Yet apparently, when it came to some certain things, why were they filled with such unbelief? Were these people not Full-Gospel – an interchangeable term for Pentecostal or Holiness – all holding the same values since the resurgence of the full truth of the Gospel through revivalist movements within various small churches in the Unicoi Mountains or at the long-lasting Spirit-filled revival at Apostolic Faith Gospel Mission – located at 312 Azusa Street, Los Angeles, California – where GOD in His perfect wisdom used a black preacher to do what many white ministers had failed to do? Various other movements had taken place to do the same thing at the same time for this latter-day outpouring. As the Apostle Peter had stated on the day of Pentecost – "This is that spoken by the Prophet Joel." And yet, calling themselves Full-Gospel did they reject the Great Commission to rain down Hellfire on the Kingdom of the enemy? Were they so blindly ignorant to think that if they'd just leave the devil alone, he'd leave them alone too? The church has a power that many don't understand it has, and when some bear witness to this power, like the holiness of GOD it drives them from Him rather than to him, for they only have a knowledge or experience instead of true intimacy with The Father of Light, in whom there is no variance or shadow of turning.

Between this time and the camp meeting in Atlanta, Pastor Jackie had Todd Driscoll up to speak twice. His first of those two sermons revolved around the account of Jesus Christ walking along the top of the stormy sea. There the waves crashed some fifty feet high around them. The disciples were afraid. In the presence of the miraculous and Christ's holiness, they shuddered. These were a lot who – after Jesus fed a vast multitude of what was perceivably 10,000 people, including women and children, with a couple of fishes and few loaves of bread – fretted thereafter because they didn't feel they'd brought enough food for another one of their journeys. With GOD literally walking in the flesh among them, the miraculous happened constantly, and yet they were shocked at the miraculous. And while it sounds a bit ridiculous that anyone might be such a fool, it is highly evident that believers in Jesus Christ are not so different today. The same GOD who heals and answers prayers gets doubted that He'll do it again. Profoundly, Brother Todd went on to say how when you invite The LORD into your life He will do things that are outside of your box.

His second sermon followed after the passage where the Apostle Paul talked about how he would preach Christ crucified. Certainly, this was all well and good. As Pastor Jackie and any discerning person would know, deliverance is merely a byproduct of the relational presence of Jesus Christ. Because you've been born again, this liberty is open to you – and yet, Betty Sue Riley and the Walls had left them...

Finally, the Monday morning had come that he'd been waiting for. Jackie and Penny got up early, packed the car, and hauled Judy and Paul Gibson down there with them. While this was so, the Nobles would be sharing a room with their long-time friends and fellow ministers of the Gospel of Jesus Christ, Reverend

Bert and Eve Massengale, who'd traveled there all the way from Oklahoma. While Bert wasn't licensed through the same organization as Pastor Jackie, the two of them were a part of the same body of Christ and likeminded. Specifically, their affiliation was with Oral Roberts, who had a church and Christian college where they lived.

Their reunion was grand. So many old friends whom they'd not seen in so long seemed to be waiting around every corner in the hotels, restaurants, and the convention center that was rented out each year for this massive gathering, as well as just about any other place that you could name, with the exclusion of public swimming pools and the like. As the Nobles and Massengales entered into where the convention was being held, many of their brothers and sisters in Christ – and particularly, several ministers in christ – were out there shaking hands, hugging necks, and in some cases, selling their gospel music albums, books they'd written, gospel tracts, Sunday-school resources, and the like.

Then, calling out to Jackie with nothing less than an elevated scream of a voice, the boisterous evangelist Harold Sizemore strove to get his attention.

"There's the pastor of Souls Harbor Holiness Church right there! C'mon on over here, Preacher Jackie. Some of these boys want to meet you! Yessir, I've been traveling these old roads from daylight to dawn, bringing the Gospel with me everywhere that I go and preaching everywhere that I'm asked. Hurry up, brother – we're waiting on you! Anyhow, back a few weeks ago I was up at some negro church…" he continued to drone on, elevating his voice from loud to extremely loud when calling out to Jackie, though from fifty feet away, he was so loud just talking to these men that he might as well be in your ear, but they all seemed to love it; as for Jackie Noble – not so much.

"A nigger church?" one asked him.

"Nigger, negro, colored…even negroid, I think… Ah! Anyhow – them's just different words for the same thing, but low and behold, I was there. I was just trying to be obedient to The LORD, you understand," he said affirmingly, slapping the one on the back with a loud cracking noise before carrying on with his self-indulgent and racist story.

"So you see, the sign over their church house door said that they believed in holiness, so I thought – I don't mind if I do – but they don't believe it like we believe it," he said.

"That so?" one brother asked.

"Sure 'nough. Some of those ladies in there had dresses without sleeves and painted toes," he explained as if he was describing a scene out of a horror movie.

"My, my," one man answered, shaking his head with distaste for the aesthetic.

"It's the truth. When I pulled up, there was some coal-black nigger there on the front porch with a wad of tobacco in 'is lip. Then he spit it out. It was the nastiest thing. I thought he must've come to get saved," he continued with a sort of Southern bravado that made the whole conversation palatable and engaging to the men and growing crowd of listeners shuffling in.

"It's the God-honest truth, but I'll tell you one thing that I didn't see coming…" he told them while looking back and forth to gauge their reactions and build anticipation before the dramatic closing of his tale.

Then there it came with him announcing, after all of that, the man who was dipping tobacco on the front porch of that negro church was their pastor. The fellows carried on about that for a few moments more. Likewise, they'd continue to spread it around and bring others to hear the strange experience that Rev. Harold Sizemore had at a negro church, but before it could go much further in the here and now, Harold directed the men around him to Pastor Jackie Noble and made introductions.

"Fellows, this right here is Pastor Jackie Noble. He is the shepherd over the flock at Souls Harbor Holiness Church here in the great state of Georgia," he said.

"Seems like I've heard of that," one man said, not having time to say much else before Harold laid a firm grasp onto the reins of this conversation and directed it as he saw fit.

"I hear that you cast a devil out of a crazed boy on a school bus. Folks have been saying that they read about it in some newspaper. I just wanted to let you know that I'm proud of you, Pastor Jack. Lord knows if I ever had a true brother in Christ Jesus, it was you," he added, hugging Jackie's neck.

This all went on for a bit longer. It was Penny who dutifully broke it up. As they walked away from Harold, who was still hollering out blessings and cordialities over

Pastor Jackie, Penny asked whether he seemed more full of it than usual. Jack kind of gave her a half smile and answered that it was all about the same; it's just that being away from some people for a while can make a person remember them better than they were. She smiled back at him as though the two of them had a joke that they alone were in on.

Brother Sizemore – who seemed appropriately named as he was a rather large man – would be there rubbing elbows with just about everyone. It was at this camp meeting that he attained a great many committed appointments for evangelistic revival meetings, homecoming celebrations, and so forth, for the next twelve months until the next one of these things rolled along. He did have a certain likability about him if you didn't know him. The problem was just that – Jackie knew him. Here a preacher, and there a preacher met up with Penny and Jack, conversing with them, saying how good it was to see them again. A few times during the week, Jackie would be asked about casting a devil out of that boy on an old abandoned school bus. It was those other things that they didn't know – and for that he was glad. At this time, he just wanted to push all of the heartache back and come into the presence of The LORD.

Monday evening's service began with a bang. Among the songs that were sung, it felt like the singers sang "Ain't No Grave" for an hour and forty-five minutes. It was a thick, saturating Spirit. Old brother Dudson's coattail went to rippling like a flag in a gale-force wind. That night, their General Overseer, Bishop Eugene Truelove, got up and preached the glory down. The contents of his sermon revolved around the forty-seventh chapter of Ezekiel, where he had a dream in which a river of water flowed out of the temple. As he'd gone a certain distance, the water was ankle deep; a ways farther and it was to the knees; even farther out, it was waist deep. And so onward Ezekiel journeyed, delving out further and further into the deep things of GOD so much so that one would have to swim in it, but no man would be able to cross.

By way of this illustration, Bishop Truelove told the people how there are some who are happy getting no further in than ankle deep with GOD. He gave analogies, and painted word pictures of what this might look like, then he talked about how some are only happy to be knee deep and so forth. The further into the sermon that he got, the more anticipation there was that something was about to happen. And so, like any skillful orator, he built and built until he got to the place where he told the congregation that he wanted to be caught up so much in the overflow that – just like Simon Peter – our LORD Jesus Christ would have to reach down to lift him up to walk atop the waves with our King. The reaction was electric that night.

On the second night, Evangelist G. M. Stone preached. His message also encompassed the Prophet Ezekiel, however in this story, he stood in a valley full of bones, as though there had been a great battle. Then The LORD called out to Ezekiel, asking him whether these dry bones could live again. Ezekiel responded – "Thou knows, Lord" – to which GOD told him to prophesy to the bones. With that, the mighty rushing wind of the Holy Ghost came through and revived them. Bones began to shake and snap together, muscles and sinews began to form. All of this went on until they were alive again by the power of Holy Ghost revival.

"You can't be touched by the Holy Ghost and be a dead church! Do you know that the same word used for 'wind' in Hebrew is the same word as they use for 'spirit'? In the Bible, it tells us that when GOD came down into the garden to walk with Adam and Eve, it was in the cool of the evening. Imagine saints, as soon as the wind settled in the trees from the entry of the Holy Ghost of GOD, they knew that The LORD of the host of Heaven had come down. Why, I know that we're inside a building, but I swear that I thought I just felt a gust of something running up and down my spine. Do you feel the Holy Ghost in this place tonight, Church? Can you feel..."

– and just like that, G. M. Stone did what one might call a triple somersault and went to running at full speed around the auditorium, not once, not twice, but three times – and he wasn't alone.

Besides this, the altar services were passionate and meaningful. Some people left rock-'n'-roll 8-tracks on the altar, others: degraded packs of cigarettes. One woman who came in with a walker unmercifully beat it to pieces on the side of the platform, crying out how she was healed, and then she began to dance. There was shouting with jubilation and tears.

Wednesday night was as it had been for years: devoted to being a youth night. The young preacher, Ryan Richards, was the speaker that night, and he did just as fine of a job as any of the older men. While he was a young man, still in his teens, he preached like a seasoned veteran. From the beginning of the conference until the end, a large banner hung overhead that read the words: "BE YE HOLY," with a scripture verse listed in far smaller font beneath the

exceedingly stout black letters on the white banner. It was the theme of this year's camp meeting and, thereby, the theme of every message at its core and the word that Brother Ryan brought was no exception. The Tuesday before delivering a dynamic word that evening, he'd receive his ordination papers instead of a mere expositor's license, and in addition was elected to serve as their Assistant National Youth Director at the side of Rev. Bill Hammond. More specifically, Brother Ryan's message was on housing the presence of GOD in our lives. Therein, he spoke of Obed-Edom and how after David tried to return the ark of the covenant of The LORD to Israel on a cart – instead of being carried on poles by priests and so forth as GOD had prescribed – a man named Uzzah stretched for his hand to stabilize the ark, to keep it from falling to the ground, and died from the power and the glory of GOD on the spot.

"You see, in the mind of this man, touching the ground would taint The Ark of GOD, but his thinking was wrong. The ground wouldn't have corrupted it at all. The prohibition was that it not be touched by the hands of man. How many of y'all know in this place today that The LORD GOD Most High can do anything? He's a GOD that never fails. He's a GOD whose ways are not our ways. And He's a GOD who is never wrong. Yet, people are so fundamentally ignorant that they want to argue with this GOD who gave them the capacity to argue in the first place.

Church, GOD is not the one that messed up the world – man is. If our wisdom could get us out of it we'd be out, but look all around. We're still fighting a war in Vietnam that has been going on for nearly 20 years! Georgia Abortions are at an all-time high! What the world is calling a sexual

revolution is a perversion of the gift of sex that GOD gave us. The worldly women of today have looked back at the men and said how they've been mindless fools – hopping in bed with one person and then with another – and the women were right! But instead of dealing with it in any kind of a right way, many of them have chosen to whore themselves out just like the men are – but at a greater cost.

Right now, the liberal paper of this city, Atlanta – named as "The Great Speckled Bird" after an old time gospel music song – is advertising that women can have abortions in this state up to twenty-four weeks into their pregnancies, and Georgia state governor Jimmy Carter isn't about to do anything to stop it.

Just one month ago, the conservative Democratic Presidential Candidate, Governor George Wallace, who held a strong chance of victory, was shot to death during his campaign. Weeks later, eight GOD-hating, Jew-hating Palestinian nationalists opened fire on the Israeli Olympic team in what the news media has dubbed 'The Munich Massacre!' But I'm here to tell you that just as firm as GOD's covenant is with Israel, GOD's covenant is with you. They're still the apple of His all-seeing eye. They're still called unto repentance and to bring salvation to the world. And as you and I know, salvation did come through Israel by this long-awaited, long-sought-for Messiah and King. How many of you know that I'm talking about Jesus?

Listen now, just like The Ark of The Covenant of GOD supernaturally changed the atmosphere within the house of Obed-Edom, the presence of GOD can change your life today. Do you know that after David brought back The Ark and danced before The LORD with all of his might, and when scripture begins to list those who labored in the house of GOD – that one of those men was Obed-Edom? That man and his family just couldn't stand to live without the presence. They couldn't stand to do without the presence. And, honey, when you know what it is to have a real relationship with Him, you won't be able to live without His presence either!

I'm tired of these preachers who are Daddy called and Mommy sent. If GOD hasn't called you, just don't go! You can't just live any old way and have GOD in your house! You can't just do any old thing and have GOD in your house! You're in the presence of the King! C'mon and praise Him like you mean it!" the young preacher declared with applause and much worship going on throughout the entire discourse of his sermon.

Certainly, the Reverend Ryan Richardson was an up-and-comer in their organization. He was being mentored and ushered in by a small yet prestigious wealth of holiness preachers within their ranks. One of whom was the well-known Bishop Bill Hammond, who'd actually nominated this younger brother to work at his side. Just like in the secular world, people often seemed to get opportunities in the church due to nepotism: who their friends were and the like. And while perhaps this might have been the case with Jackie Noble, the overlying evidence that there were so many other

people that the board and even his friend Byron Phillips could have chosen made it feel like more of a GOD thing, though each and every one of them would credit The LORD whether He discernibly had anything to do with them getting in office or not. They'd quote what Jesus said to Pilate and things of that nature. Regardless, GOD was still very much in charge of everything, no matter how bad people messed things up. And while Jackie Noble loved all of this good preaching, these were some hard acts to follow – as the saying goes. And while these first three nights were intense, the Wednesday and Thursday-morning services did not wane at all in scriptural integrity or power.

Generally speaking, the stylization of the morning services could go one of two ways. The organization would either have a teaching-style preacher get up for what might seem like a more "with-it" Sunday school lesson, or a lesser-known pastor would get up, leaving the pulpit of the evening services open to all of the big wigs. As what seemed almost like a rule of law, the night services tended to triple in their size of attendance. And yet throughout this meeting there seemed to be some kind of gossip as to the highly anointed demon-slaying ministry of the otherwise small Georgia town and small Georgia church country-preacher Jackie Noble, causing a few to wonder what might happen on the morning that he'd get up to speak and what would happen when he did. Really, it was a kind of pressure that he didn't need or want any part of. Trying to enjoy the good Spirit, Jackie went to every meeting.

Wednesday morning's service was preached by a more scholarly clergyman from Cleveland, Ohio. His key text was from the sixth chapter of Isaiah, wherein the Prophet was ushered into the throne room of Almighty GOD, who was high and lifted up and His train filled the temple. There around Him the angels cried, "Holy, Holy, Holy!" and in the presence and backsplash of pure and true holiness, Isaiah could see every imperfection in him – just like someone can see all of the crud on their car's windshield when the light shines through – though it is otherwise masked by the darkness. On Thursday morning, a preacher from Florida got up and preached a message revolving around the life of Moses. And then came Thursday night.

As they had been in years past, Thursday evenings were set aside for World Missions. There they'd have an international speaker – from India, Africa, South America, or some other place outside of the United States of America – get up and preach a message along the lines of that year's theme, all while conveying the harsh realities of where they lived. Thereby, this tended to be the only service that wasn't preached by a caucasian man, as caucasian men made up the overwhelming majority of the clergymen of their holiness organizations, minus a few black men up North, in Mississippi, and some Mexicans throughout Florida. That evening, a man of Latin American descent got up and began to tell his story of how he used to be a hitman in the mob, but Jesus Christ saved his soul. The courts had him dead to rights, but when it came time to put him in prison – shortly after he'd left that life and been converted – some way, somehow, all evidence that they had disappeared. He told the people how GOD can take your old life and make it new. He told them how he used to take men's lives, but now he saves them, and how he went from being a very bad man to becoming a man of GOD. It was a powerful testimony of the transformation that The LORD had caused.

That night after service, as they had done all through the week, Pastor Jackie, Penny, and an accompaniment of others went to one restaurant or another. In any such case, they were filled with various holiness people, thus bringing some of their church atmosphere out into the world, and spreading some money around from GOD's people all throughout the Atlantan economy.

This evening, at the particular restaurant where Jackie and Penny had elected to go, they also found Rev. Ryan Richardson, along with Bill Hammond, Orlando Walden, Russell Ledbetter, and Landes Stoneking (to name only a few of the bigger name preachers), all of whom had pulled multiple tables together like they owned the place. Among them at the table that seemed to have nearly forty people was his long-time pastor and friend, Dr. Byron Phillips, who waved Jackie, Penny, and essentially the Massingels over – as they were with them.

"Pull up another table," someone shouted, egging it on.

"Here, let me help y'all with that," Ryan Richardson accommodatingly said.

The young man seemed to have a servant's heart. He carried himself like pure gold. During the evening he'd both break down scripture and innumerate a long list of sinful things going on in the world – almost as if he was trying to convince everyone how knowledgeable he was – though he did it all in a way that seemed so sincere as to be without reproof.

He talked about the shooting at the Olympics, that July's Gay Pride Parade down on Peach Street in Atlanta, all of the worldly bands that Howard Stern had

been bringing to their city – such as Black Sabbath, the Velvet Underground, and such. He likewise knew of the immoral movies that came out that year, like *Fritz The Cat*, an X-rated animated cartoon, and Stanley Kubrick's film, *A Clockwork Orange*, which the ads and movie poster described as – "Being the adventures of a young man whose principal interests are rape, ultra-violence and Beethoven." Nevertheless, after having multiple conversations with multiple people who'd otherwise never seemed to pay him much mind, Jackie sincerely began to think to himself that this could be a door opening to new things. Perhaps from here on out he'd be speaking at more conferences and such – if he did well. This whole affair lasted nearly three hours, sending them to bed late. Penny and Jackie rose early in the morning. Like them, the Massingales were both coffee drinkers. They went through a restaurant drive-through and got a few cups, some small breakfast sandwiches to eat on the way and from there on out, they were off to arrive at the morning meeting early. When they arrived, Jackie went into the men's room to splash some water on his face and there, following the sound of a toilet's flush, Harold Sizemore exited a stall. After washing and drying his hands, he reached into his inner breast pocket and pulled out a bag of his coveted breath-freshening candy – if candy is the word.

> "Sen-Sen?" he asked, holding the bag open towards Pastor Jackie as though implying that he ought to take some.

Afraid that perhaps he should, Jackie told him thanks and held open his hand for Brother Sizemore to drop out a few shreds of the gingery flakes. Then, taking some more for himself – who'd already had quite a bit of it based on the gingery smell of his breath – he said how it was just like manna from Heaven.

Leaving the bathroom, Pastor Jackie found himself talking with this person and then that. He spoke and shook hands with all of the other speakers that week, all of the ministers with whom he'd sat last night, and far too many others to name. Both clergymen and lay folk all seemed to want to say hello. After all of his faithful years in ministry this might very well be his moment in the sun. To keep the flow of things going, the board who put this grand assembly together also selected an array of singers and musicians to alternate throughout the duration of camp-meeting. In a general sense they were the same ones – so to keep a balance to it all, but they did slightly mix it up here and there so nobody would feel like they were getting over-exposure. Sister Tammy Cornelius served as the worship leader on that Friday morning. She was a highly anointed woman of GOD whose hair stood stacked every bit as high as the tower of Babel. However much hairspray she had on it seemed to be doing the job, as from observing her, it was questionable whether or not a tornado might be able to shift that up-do that she had going on there.

Had Jackie been sitting with his wife, Penny probably would have jested – asking him whether he thought that she ought to wear her hair like that – to which he answered in his head how he didn't know that they could afford the upkeep. Finding the imaginary conversation somewhat funny, he exhibited a half smile and then looked out to his wife – who darlingly crinkled her nose at him as if to say – "I love you." Correcting his expression, Pastor Noble then began to focus on The LORD as Sister Cornelius led off the Friday morning worship with the song, "How Great Thou Art." She did a marvelous job, not that any person alone could be given the glory for the sensational feeling that swept across the auditorium as she sang. Several more wondrous gospel songs followed. Everybody seemed to sing along with

her as she sang "Give Me That Old-Time Religion." Then, finally, she ended in singing "Something Got a Hold of Me," which goes:

SOMETHING GOT A HOLD OF ME

1ST VERSE:

When first I heard of a people who claimed
This old time religion was real
I said I'll go down and look at the crowd
It's just the weak minded I feel

CHORUS:

But something got a hold of me
Yes something got a hold of me
I went there to fight but on that night
There's something got a hold of me

2ND VERSE:

I went right down to sit at the door
And the devil said don't you go in
I said I'll go in for that cannot hurt
And sit as far back as I can

3RD VERSE:

About that time he got up to leave
And he looked right down upon me
He told everybody how mean I had been
Not thinking so much of me

4TH VERSE:

They sing and shout and they all clapped their hands
And they all got down on their knees
When the fire came from heaven it fell right on me
And then I fell to the floor

5TH VERSE:

So now I've learnt and there's no need to doubt
That the old time religion is real
I have a spirit I'll never forget
That something got a hold of me

Approaching the microphone, directly after Sister Cornelius finished singing that song, was Dr. Byron Phillips. Across the auditorium, people were praising the LORD. Some were crying tears. Others shaking under the power of the Holy Ghost as they lifted their hands and rocked back and forth like a candle's flame dancing in the breeze.

"Well, Glory! I know that the world doesn't have anything like what we just heard here today. She's not only a fine singer but an anointed singer too. Praise GOD. For those of you who've looked at our camp meeting schedule – it announced that we were going to have Pastor Warren Young up to preach this morning, but due to a family emergency, he was unable to be here. It's all right, though. He tells me that Margaret is doing fine and they're now the proud parents of a healthy baby boy, Moses Josiah Young. Whew! And with a name like that, I can't even imagine that boy being anything other than a preacher, can you? Hallelujah!

Well, with no further ado, I'd like to welcome to the podium a young man who formerly served as my youth pastor. Since then, he's pastored here in the great state of Georgia, marched outside of Abortion Clinics, and most recently, cast out a devil from a wild-eyed drug addict living in an old   abandoned school bus. My brothers and sisters in Christ, won't you please give a warm welcome to our dear brother Pastor Jackie Noble?" Dr. Phillips said, then hugging Jackie as he handed him the microphone and telling him with a smile to preach them happy, as he turned loose and walked back to his seat on the stage.

Jackie's eyes combed over the audience of what appeared to be something around 2,000 people. Of these were his highly esteemed clergymen, deacons, missionaries, their wives and children, as well as all sorts of other church folks looking to get something from GOD. Moreover, this morning they were looking for Jackie Noble to give it to them. Thereby, opening his Bible to the text that he had marked with a piece of notebook paper, which also had his sermon notes on it, he cleared his throat and pressed forward into his message.

"I began attending New Life Fellowship Church when I was just a young preacher attending Atlanta Bible College. Dr. Byron was still there at that time and had been there quite some time before that. His advice to me way back then was to 'get up, speak up, and shut up.' Seeing as how he's a man of set convictions, I don't suppose his thoughts on that have ever changed. …so that is just what I'm aiming to do today," he said, grinning and looking out of the corner of his eye at Dr. Phillips and the other high-up ministers who were nearly falling over, slapping their legs laughing.

He then asked them to turn in their Bibles to the Gospel of Mark in the eleventh chapter and then began to complement how wonderful everyone and everything had been thus far at the meeting. Further, he thanked the board and Dr. Phillips for the distinct privilege to minister at their annual camp-meeting. After all of this, he directed all who were able to please stand as an act of reverence to GOD's word and thus he read.

"'And on the morrow, when they were come from Bethany, he was hungry: And seeing a fig tree afar off having leaves, he came, if haply he

might find any thing thereon: and when he came to it, he found nothing but leaves; for the time of figs was not yet. And Jesus answered and said unto it, No man eat fruit of thee hereafter for ever. And his disciples heard it.'"

– MARK 11:12-14

He went on to briefly talk about the events of that chapter. Before this series of verses, the disciples got a donkey who had never been ridden for Christ to enter into Jerusalem. Those who had coats would lay them out before him, so that it might walk on them. Those who were too poor would gather palm branches. Whereas riding a horse is emblematic of one riding into battle, it is said that judges rode donkeys. Moreover, a donkey is emblematic of a burden bearer.

Many believed that their long-awaited king had come; that he was the Messiah. Hence they cried "hosannah" – which is to say – transliterated into English: "Save us now." Contrasting this, the Roman, Pontius Pilate, entered the city at another gate. Everyone who celebrated who they thought Jesus of Nazareth was had things figured out in their heads, whereas really He was far greater and far more than they ever could have imagined. On the next day, came this passage that Pastor Jackie had read.

"After this, GOD's judgment begins at His house. Jesus entered into the temple and saw merchants selling and reselling sacrificial animals. This is exactly the type of reasoning why the Prophets Isaiah, Amos, and Jeremiah all spoke a "Thus sayeth The LORD word in expression for GOD's complete disdain for the very practices that He'd initiated – for The Church had polluted them. After setting loose doves, strongly rebuking

the degenerate hypocrites in the temple, and so forth. Upon leaving, Christ and his disciples came upon the fig tree that he'd cursed on the previous day and they marveled at how it had withered. On that particular instance, He answered them in regards of how if they had faith the size of a mustard seed that they could say to that mountain – an impossibly immovable thing – to be removed and cast into the sea, and it would. Thereby, the order of the chapter is this: Christ inwardly being everything that He should be. The fig tree externally appearing to be something that it was not, for it bore no fruit and subsequently was damned by GOD. The church failing to be what they were called to be and being cast out of the place of the presence of The LORD. And finally, that thing that was not as it seemed being annihilated."

He explained how he didn't wear short sleeves, wedding bands, and forbade himself to do a grand number of other things, just like many of his other brothers and sisters in the congregation, because of a sincere conviction inside of him.

"It's what's on the inside of me that branches out to the outside of me. We're called to let the light within us shine for the whole wide world to see," he declared.

Moreover, Pastor Jackie talked about how there were people who just played church. He emphasized how many of these preachers that were in the service with them – who knew all of the church language, who knew when to shout, and who knew all the same songs – could rather easily put on an act. Like that fig tree that bore no fruit, from a distance you'd think that they were real. It's only become obvious by being really close to them and examining that their life does bear the fruit or testify that they're the thing they're pretending to be. And while our works don't save us, you will know a tree by the fruit that it bears.

"We become like what we worship. Those things influence us. The early church were called Christians to deride them. It was meant as a slur and yet a great complement. Essentially, people were saying that those guys acted just like Jesus Christ. Wouldn't that be something? Wouldn't it be wonderful if the world saw Jesus Christ modeled in everyone of you?

Integrity is what you do and who you are when nobody else is watching – or you think nobody else is watching. Do you think that GOD ever stops to laugh at a dirty joke? Do you think that GOD ever takes occasion to be anything other than holy? Of course not, and we're called to be holy, just like Him, for without holiness, no man shall see GOD," Pastor Jackie hollered out explosively into the microphone.

It was all being taken quite well by everybody. One person even dashed up to the altar to pray as though it was out of a desperation that couldn't wait for an altar call. Of course, this is how church should always be done. The altars should always be open. After all, people who'd go to the altar – unless it was merely out of show, like the fig tree Jackie spoke of – were led by the loving conviction of The Holy Ghost to do so.

There was such a grace and power flowing in that Friday morning's service. Jackie Noble felt as though he could walk on air. After giving a heartfelt invitation for

any to come to the altar who needed a closer walk with GOD, who wanted to put on true holiness, who needed a refreshing, and likewise, any who'd never committed themselves unto The LORD to begin with to come. Thus far everything was quite normal – that is, until a young lady by the name of Hannah Ledbetter approached Pastor Jackie for prayer. Of course, he recognized her and was more than happy to pray with her. She was the daughter of Rev. Russell Ledbetter, who was sitting at the table with Jackie, Penny, and the others just the night before. Moreover, Russell Ledbetter was a regular "who's who" of the preachers there. He was the pastor of one of their organization's largest churches, located in the state of Alabama. They gave an enormity to missions, the Smoky Mountain Pentecostal Children's Home – for orphans of Barboursville, Kentucky – and so forth. If ever there was someone somewhat prestigious that Jackie Noble, and he alone, had been personally asked to pray over, it was this child, due to who her daddy was.

In response to Jackie questioning that she elaborate about the specific need, Hannah Ledbetter came in close – in fact, so close that no one else would hear her. She was a wholesome looking girl, befitting of a holiness pastor's daughter. She was probably no more than fourteen or fifteen years old. And yet, the worrisome look on her face told some kind of a story that Jackie felt needed elaboration.

His concern for her was very real. Jackie Noble was a true pastor, called of GOD, empathizing with others and wanting to see them set free from whatever thing it was that plagued them – and so he heard her request.

"I've heard people talking about you, preacher. They say that you have the power to cast out demons. Please help me," she said.

Jackie gave her a slight smile in a caring sort of way. Surely this girl must have been mistaken if she thought, by any means, that she might have had a demon. Perhaps all of this talk about the school-bus exorcism had gotten this girl's young mind in that kind of a mode. She was searching for answers and had come to one of the gravest conclusions possible.

"Tell me what's the matter," he kindly said – hoping that this information might lead him down a rabbit trail towards finding the real root cause to her affliction.

With tear-filled eyes, this trembling young church girl – the daughter of a prominent holiness Pastor – quietly told the reverend that she desperately needed prayer because she just couldn't stop masturbating. Somewhat shocked to hear this from her, Jackie Noble stretched out his hand toward the child and began to pray.

"Lord, in the name of Jesus Christ, I actively call out and cast out this spirit of masturbation, this spirit of perversion, and every foul thing," exclaimed Jackie with his voice elevating more and more as he prayed, though he did not mean to yell.

And with that, all of Hell seemingly broke loose – as it is to say. Something from inside of this teenage girl with a voice far from her own began to cry perversities and profanities and sexualized rantings all throughout – claims it stated that it had on her. While some people were up front praying, this whole episode was so intense that it began to attract the attention from more and more people across the auditorium in a growing succession. Seeing as how this was no small affair, but a sizable convocation, several ministers came in to aid

and usher the prominent pastor's daughter into one of the conference rooms in the building. During this time, he'd actually left to go to the restroom, thereby keeping him from witnessing the scene that was being made by his own flesh-and-blood daughter. Still, all of these men knew who she was as Pastor Russell Ledbetter was regarded as a very important man.

Trying to save face and keep some semblance of order, the Reverend Doctor Byron Phillips – the man that Pastor Jackie regarded as his pastor, mentor, and friend – took up the microphone and reigned the service back in with oratory precision. Essentially, he told the people not to worry, that they had a host of well-trained ministers who were getting that young lady help and that everything was fine – although he knew that what was going on there and then was anything but a commonality. Moreover, during the men's time back in a conference room with Pastor Ledbetter's daughter, Rev. Harold Sizemore was brought up on stage to help keep things going smoothly by sermonizing, praying, and singing altar-service type songs. Of them, he began by singing, "Reach Out and Touch the Lord."

Meanwhile, havoc ensued in the conference room as the girl wept violently, flailing and trying to attack the surrounding ministers who had to restrain her from hitting or scratching. Within this whole instance, men were trying to reason with the girl, Preachers asking in an accusatory manner what Jackie Noble did to her, as well as perpetually every off-kilter response around those lines. One moment they asked him to leave, but then as the girl screamed and wailed – calling specifically for him to save her – they let him back into the room that he was cast out of for what might have felt like the longest two minutes of his life.

Once he was back in the room, Jackie began to question the evil presence within Hannah Ledbetter. Whereas it had said that it had rights, he asked how it had gotten there. To this, the demon divulged that it came into her from looking at her father's pornographic magazines. The men in there reacted in a sense that they were completely appalled at everything that was happening. Nevertheless in about twenty to twenty-five minutes' time, Pastor Jackie felt that he had thoroughly cast the devil out of her through the authoritative power of Jesus Christ, through the Holy Ghost. Finally, at that point she was sitting and acting normal, though a bit shaken.

One of the men gave her a box of tissues with which to dry her eyes and nose. Another two men in there left with Jackie Noble being escorted likewise.

"We'll handle it from here," said the officiating preacher – General Assistant Overseer, Bishop Orlando Walden.

He was there, left with the girl and two other men, alone in the room. As they – Jackie and the other two of the six who were in there – walked away from the room and back towards the auditorium, her father, Russell Ledbetter, rounded the corner in a fit of concern – which looked a bit more like angered frustration. One of the two men answered his question as to where his daughter was by guiding him to the room and thereafter guarding the door to keep others away. Meanwhile, the other minister, who was with Jack, almost guided him away as one might an unruly little yapping dog. Jackie Noble had never seen and heard something so magnificent and altogether offsetting as he had in that room. A high-ranking minister within their organization was consumed with a burning sexual lust. From the best that he could

tell, these weren't even normal pornographic magazines that he had – but something much more vile in their presentation. Yet, it was almost if Jackie was being looked at like a creep.

Jackie withdrew himself, heading towards the sounds of praying, and music. He could hear Reverend Sizemore's enormous voice ring out like a bell as he sang:

> "Plenty of time to decide where I'm bound
> To Eternal darkness or to a Heavenly Crown.
> I'm just a young man – Not yet in my prime.
> So I'll just wait – I've got plenty of time."

He was nearing the end of it by the virtue of the verse that he landed on next. Another preacher was up at the same time, calling for the lost to come and be saved. And as he walked in the door, Dr. Byron Phillips took him by the arm and asked Jackie to come with him so that they could talk alone.

Somewhat privately, in a foyer area, Jackie told his mentor and friend what was going on, both with her having a demon inside of her and the thing saying that this all happened because she was looking at her father's pornography. Dr. Byron acted exactly how he should in some regard, while in other ways, he was trying to be on cleanup detail. After all, he was the one who'd pressed for them to have Jackie Noble up to preach; therefore, he acted as though he felt somewhat responsible.

To that he said, "I'm just sorry that all of this happened."

And while making that statement over an occasion when a young girl gets set free should require some sort of explanation – none was given. This all unwound in a way where Penny, Jackie, and the Massingales went out for lunch. Knowing the couple for such a long time, Jackie felt comfortable sharing in front of them exactly what had happened. They all then went out shopping, though he felt odd and somewhat shafted after an otherwise terrific service. Upon returning that evening for church, Rev. Landes Walden, along with two other men, met Pastor Jackie at the door and told him that due to the earlier events in the day, he'd have to ask him to leave. Rather than argue with them, Jackie and Penny returned to the hotel to get their things, as they now planned to leave for home early. Thereby, they had word sent to Judy and Paul Gibson, who left the evening service before it began, knowing that some extraordinary situation must be going on to cause the Nobles to get up and dash back home at a moment's notice.

With the other couple in the car – Jackie partially wanted to cry and partially was too upset to even do that. Like his coffee pot coming to a boil, Pastor Noble stewed and stewed and finally let it all out. There, for a long period of time, he expressed his grief and disbelief at what had happened and how he was being treated. Moreover, he wondered what was being said and done behind the scenes that led to them asking him to leave. As it turned into a group discussion of sorts, it still wasn't the sort of matter that he really felt like continuing to talk about for the duration of the trip. It both grieved him and rattled him so much that a part of him wondered if he had done anything wrong at all.

It was 11:45 p.m. when the Nobles' phone rang. Dr. Byron Phillips had a conversation with Jackie, telling him that there had been some sort of ministers' meeting

going on and they were determining what to do about everything that happened. While this left many whys and other such questions, he also called to tell Jackie that he'd talk to him when he saw him on Sunday morning. He insisted that he'd be coming down to the church to preach – that New Life Fellowship Church had it all covered – and that the two of them were going to spend some time together so that they could get this whole thing worked out in a way that was better for everyone. After Dr. Phillips hung up the phone, Jackie just continued to sit there listening to the dead, cold flatline sound until it pulsed like a heartbeat. Then and there, feeling more alone than he might ever have felt, Jackie Noble began to sob.

Penny got up out of bed, walked into the room, took the phone from his hand, hung it up, and held her grieving husband and pastor – telling him how GOD had this whole situation under control.

CHAPTER 07

Sunday Morning
Coming Down

Saturday came and went with a few phone calls in between from church members, inquiring about what exactly happened on Friday morning of their annual Pentecostal convocation that caused Pastor Jackie, Sister Penny and the Gibsons to leave the camp meeting early. Another call informed them that two other papers outside the state of Georgia found out about the article in their local paper and essentially reran the story of the school-bus exorcism due to the extraordinary nature of it all.

"If only they knew the rest of what was happening," Penny responded to Jackie, concerning the matter.

"I know. That's right," he answered agreeingly – the way one might when their heart has been deeply wounded.

Whereas it would normally be a grand pleasure to have his beloved friend and pastor – the great Dr. Byron Phillips – down to speak and visit at his little country holiness church, this whole affair seemed forced, like a friend coming as a messenger to deliver a rebuke, and it was in every way unpleasant. Jackie and Penny's only recourse was to take this battle before The LORD and lay it at the foot of the cross. Oh, how they prayed. They asked the others to whom they talked that they likewise

pray. As the sun came up the next morning – Sunday, September 24th, 1972 – it was all that Jackie Noble could do to drink three cups of coffee before heading to the church house early to sweep, dry mop, tidy, and dust, along with his faithful few.

Due to their early arrival, he informed the cleaning committee as to what was going on. While they often took playful jabs at one another, Sister Young was one of the pastor's truest friends and most faithful supporters. She expressed her sincere sympathies, her hopes that everything would work out just fine, and in saying so, gave him the one-armed church hug that was neither too light of a touch nor so much that one person was pressing into the other but just enough to know that someone cares about you.

Dr. Phillips slipped into Souls Harbor Holiness Church early into the Sunday school lesson, in which he participated a bit and likewise listened attentively. The people who knew him – which was the majority – were more than enthused to see him there visiting, except for those who were privy that this visitation might not be for the best of reasons. They surmised that the organization had sent someone who'd be extremely well received and without rebuke to issue a heavy yet skillful blow to the man of GOD who had faithfully served them for so many years. Besides Dr. Byron Phillips' general prestige, he also had the benefit of personally meeting all but the newer congregants as he'd been there on two separate occasions to honor his friend, Jackie Noble, on each of those pastor-appreciation days. This time, however, stood in complete contrast, for on both of those happy occasions, he had brought both his wife Joyce and a nurse to help her while he preached. This time, he had come alone.

When asked, he assured people that both his wife and sizable church were being taken good care of. While it was uncertain what had caused her ailment, medical doctors diagnosed her condition as Lou Gehrig's disease. During Jackie Noble's time serving at New Life Fellowship, her health was fine. The symptoms of that which afflicted her had only been present for the last few years. Perhaps in the spirit of what had been going on with all of the exorcisms and deliverance ministry at their church, Brother Tony Edwards' lesson was centered around MARK 9:38-41 which reads as follows:

> "'And John answered him, saying, Master, we saw one casting out devils in thy name, and he followeth not us: and we forbad him, because he followeth not us. But Jesus said, Forbid him not: for there is no man which shall do a miracle in my name, that can lightly speak evil of me. For he that is not against us is on our part. For whosoever shall give you a cup of water to drink in my name, because ye belong to Christ, verily I say unto you, he shall not lose his reward.'"

This passage was an abundantly clear message from the lips of Jesus Christ, who in essence was coming against intolerance within the church over one variation in thought or another – right or wrong. After all, there were only two kinds of people in the world: saved and unsaved. Likewise, there were a staggering list of things that a person could be completely wrong about doctrinally that would have no bearing on their salvation; case in point – fully understanding the Holy Trinity, discerning the time of the rapture of the church, immersion versus sprinkling during baptism, and so on an so forth. Even the book of the Revelation of John tells us in the open letter to the seven churches that there will still be some people in those churches that are wrong about a great many things – overall, on their way to Hell – who are saved. It is very possible to be a Christian who is Catholic, Baptist, Methodist, Presbyterian, and so on and so forth. Likewise, there are people who attend church for tradition, for community, or for any other reason besides having a more intimate relationship with GOD: iron sharpening iron, and such.

Therefore, whether it be Baptists who feel some sort of unholy calling to bash Pentecostals, the anti-musical instrumental Church of Christ saying that they're the only ones who are going to make it, the Oneness Pentecostal Jesus-Onlies claiming that they're the only ones and that salvation is conducive with manifesting the infilling of the Holy Ghost by speaking in tongues – Christ instructs His followers to examine whether or not those other bear good fruit and if so, to leave them alone. Perhaps someone is farther along than the other in this great race. Howbeit, that is the very nature of a race, and the more important point isn't who is ahead of whom but whether an individual is passionately pursuing after GOD or not.

If nothing else could be said, this particular lesson on this particular day proved interesting. And while Dr. Byron interjected some sentiments, being the orator that he was, he did not slip up even once. Rather, he pointed out as to how the twelve disciples of Christ were trying to take jurisdiction over something over which they had no dominion. It was a sad reality regarding the splintering of the church body. A Baptist, rightfully or not, couldn't say anything corrective to a Roman Catholic, because if they did, the Roman Catholic would simply reply: "What do you have to do with me? I am a part of the Holy Catholic Church which is the Worldwide Church of GOD, which has come down through Apostolic succession from Saint Peter, as commissioned by our LORD Jesus Christ."

The arguments would be, likewise, here and there. Moreover, the one might say to the other: "And besides that, what about the beam in your own eye?" – to which their assertion might even be correct. Dr. Phillips further emphasized how if the Holiness church of which they were a part didn't portray holiness and all things good for doctrine, then who were they to say anything to anyone else? Thereby, this message that might put up a wall before another man – coming there for the reasons that he likely had come – were only manipulated by bending this thing and swaying that - to serve the cause of headquarters.

After Sunday school was over, Sister Eleanor approached the piano and played a hymn, lick for lick, as it was written in the book. Martha, who otherwise sang well, did the best that she could with the pianist keeping it in such an awful key for her. Being the man that he was, with a keen understanding of things, Dr. Byron lept to the pulpit and began to take over the service in such a way as to cut the fiasco that was their worship short, as well as to help the service along. While Sunday school was going on, he'd already let Pastor Jackie – as well as their lay minister – know that he meant to meet with them all directly after service. Despite what seemed a grim occasion, he acted unphased by any negativity that had surrounded it. The key text for his sermon was found within the most Pentecostal chapter in the entirety of the Bible: 1st Corinthians 14.

Whereas that entire chapter is about the administration of the gift of speaking in tongues, and has verses that say things like - "Forbid not to speak in tongues, verses on edification, verses on interpretation, and all else" - the text that he read from was the very last verse of the chapter, which read:

"Let all things be done decently and in order."

If you've ever known what it was like to get a really bad feeling about what was going to happen, then you might perhaps know how Pastor Jackie felt. While the LORD most certainly did still speak to His church, ministers also have utilized the pulpits to act as spiritual snipers. GOD forbid that anyone had done anything against their children or what have you. A certain kind of individual might take the occasion to levy their power into a form of spiritual abuse that they feel justified in using. The question was – was his mentor, pastor, and friend such a man? Had he really come to stick the knife in? His sermon was so indirect that if the man was making jabs, they were so subtle that he alone might have known it. Still, there were points to be made in the message.

One of the things that he dealt with was adhering to church authority, a point off which each subsequent point seemed to branch. It seemed all a bit too telling with what had happened that this was some sort of reproof, muted or not. He was trying to give Jackie some kind of food for thought. Howbeit, in Jackie's mind, the fact of the matter that couldn't escape him is that when Jesus Christ addressed the issue of spiritual authority, it tended to be on the other end of things – as he pointed out countless times how certain people lord over others and abuse them by means of their power. Christ's message wasn't one of blind submission but to do what is right in the sight of GOD, all while being aware of how things really were around you and not becoming like the hypocritical leadership of the day.

Finally, after about twenty-five minutes of preaching, the Reverend Doctor Byron Phillips closed with a short and eloquent prayer. The people were jointly

dismissed and informed that their headquarters took a great interest in their church and were in the midst of planning some wonderful things for them in the future. Jackie kept up a brave face, shook hands with the people, welcomed some visitors, and met a stranger who'd come from miles away. He told him that he'd read about their church in the newspaper and would be in town for a few more days. Besides this, he seemed to have a great desire to talk to the Nobles. It was somewhat noticeable to Penny that the man with curls at the end of his words, from another part of the country, had been talking with several other people, letting them know his whereabouts and getting their phone numbers. As he and Jackie talked, it was apparent that he already knew where he worked. Subsequently, the man offered to stop by during the week and have lunch with him before traveling home. Jackie agreed to lunch tomorrow. The two of them would meet at the Waffle House not too far off from the J. C. Penny's department store where he worked on Monday at noon. Shaking his hand, the fellow headed out the door and looked as though he was resuming an afore-held conversation with Paul and Judy Gibson. Whatever that was all about, it was the last thing on his mind. It seemed that Jackie and Dr. Phillips had business to attend to.

While he didn't act in any way at all that was ill, it also seemed that his dear friend, mentor, and the man whom he considered as his pastor did nothing to defend him in lieu of what was said - as well as what was not said. The long and short of it went like this: the administration was looking into the allegations concerning Pastor Russell Ledbetter, the mental stability and integrity of his teenage daughter's witness, as well as doing a thorough examination as to what exactly happened between Jackie and that girl that night.

"It was an embarrassment to the whole assembly," Dr. Phillips at one point blurted out, as though losing his composure for only a moment before reeling things back in.

Furthermore, he instructed the Nobles that due to the fragility of the circumstance, the general council felt it best that neither Pastor Ledbetter nor Pastor Noble preach in their church's pulpit during the investigation. This all seemed so utterly absurd, but no matter how much Jackie questioned the reasonability of all of this – stating again and again how things had played out to his so-called friend – the more hate-filled the conversation seemed to get. Clearly, this wasn't a request, but an order. Penny too tried to speak up, as if one could imagine a woman in this sort of complementarian environment to say anything and be received, let alone to an elder of Dr. Phillips' caliber. Nonetheless, what wound up happening is, for the time being, Jackie was asked to take a leave of absence from his pastoral station and allow for Reverend Todd Driscoll to take the reins on an interim basis or what he was told would be only a month or so. Todd answered in a way where he was somehow both apologizing to his preacher and honoring the wishes of the general council, lest they'd just gone ahead and closed the door, sending in another preacher who nobody there knew. Dismissing Rev. Driscoll, Dr. Phillips then put his hand on Jackie's shoulder firmly and told him that now that all of that was out of the way, he wanted the three of them to get a bite to eat so they could talk about other matters. Holding back the tears while nodding in agreement, Jackie accepted meeting his elder down at a local diner. He cried most of the way there.

"Sometimes I feel like Jeremiah," he said as he wiped his eyes, moments before getting out of the car.

After exiting his station wagon, hurting or not, he walked around the front of it and held Penny's door for her as he had always done. After all, life could never hit him too hard to forget how good he had it to have a wife like her. Having the front door held for them by Dr. Phillips, they each walked in, with Penny stepping into the restaurant's foyer first and then Jackie; each of whom extended a thank you. Once inside of the restaurant's foyer, Jackie held open the second door for his wife and the man who, up until this time, had been a constant source of encouragement and support for him and his ministry. Inwardly he pondered whether something had changed or if it was just a matter of him not seeing something that was in the midst of all of this chaos. Why was he being disciplined for the sins of another? Still, there was some remnant of hope within him that this meeting might dispel all of his fears. The sad truth was that Jackie Noble genuinely trusted Dr. Byron Phillips. The man had almost been a sort of a spiritual father to him – and not the sort that says to every Tom, Dick, and Harry that they're just like a son to them as a means to manipulate, despite scripture's damnation of such tactics. Byron Phillips had been there for him, and even here, recently, he presented Jackie with an opportunity that it was clear he had a hand in. Therefore, over and over in his head, Jackie kept repeating to himself to just hear the man out.

It was within ten minutes of waiting on one of the padded seats around the lobby of the restaurant that the three of them were seated. As the hostess took them back to their booth, a number of young people began to call out with cheerful greetings and salutations in the direction of Jackie Noble. One young man, along with his friend, told him how he thought it was really hip what he did for Larry a little over a month ago in that old, broken-down wreck of a school bus. Additionally, he told him that he knew Daphne Blake and she told him that he'd cast devils out of other people right in the middle of church services. With all of this, his friend chimed in, asking how often that kind of thing happens, how many exorcisms he'd performed, and all manner of other things. Jackie's answers were short and sweet. He'd say things like a few, and you'll know it when it happens. While they were imprecise they also affirmed other things that Dr. Phillips had yet to talk about to Jackie Noble. He acted kind and even pastoral toward the teenage boys. It was as to be expected. The only time that Jackie had ever seen his pastor's bedside manner come a bit undone by any account was his being heavy-handed with him down at the church – though, revisiting it, that probably wouldn't qualify. They were a wonderful source of information and confirmation, after all.

Interrupting the young men and sending them on their way was the waitress who came to take their order. Penny ordered the chicken-fried chicken, greens, and mashed potatoes. Jackie ordered a bowl of butter beans and cornbread with a side of tomatoes - to slice up and mingle with the beans and cornbread.

"My, that does sound good. I think that I'll have the butter beans and cornbread myself," Byron told the waitress.

"Would you like some tomato slices too?" she asked.

"No, thank you. That'll be all for now," he answered politely.

With those teenagers gone, the three of them were finally able to get down to business and talk about, but what more was there to say? Jackie and Penny both wondered to themselves. And there in that moment – that brief space of time before someone else would come to the table and interrupt their chat – keeping himself perfectly composed, Byron Phillip shined bright the light of who he was for Jackie Noble to see. He told him about how he'd always loved him and Penny. He spoke of how dear they were to him, and then went on to tell them that this whole thing was just some sort of bad deal.

"You've crossed the wrong people, Jack. I mean, c'mon. You must have some inkling of how big of a deal Russell Ledbetter and his five-thousand-member church is to the assembly? He basically has a lot of these guys on a string. Half of the others are related to him. You know that, don't you?" Dr. Phillips told him.

"Pastor Phillips, Jesus Christ set that girl free that night, and if that's the only good that happened from my ministering – it was well worth it," Jackie said with daring.

Penny just looked on at him in amazement. It was as though the Holy Spirit was working through him unlike ever before, even here and now. In her mind's eye she could hear the three Hebrew children from the book of Daniel answering the king in saying that they believed that The LORD would deliver them from the fiery furnace and his hand, but even if The LORD did not to let it be known, they still would not bow down before the idol that he had set up. This like that was an act of righteous defiance. Being the diplomat that he was, Dr. Phillips tried to get Jackie to let go of all of this exorcism and deliverance nonsense – as he called it. Moreover, he told him that even before the two teenage boys came to their booth, he had heard from various sources that this kind of thing had been going on pretty often with him, and it needed to stop.

> "I know you're sincere, Jackie. But a person can be sincere and wrong all at the same time. You don't want people thinking that you're a nut, do you?" Dr. Phillips finally said as if he'd come to some place of desperation where he had to dissuade the Reverend Jackie Noble – his Jackie Noble, the one whom he shaped and played such an instrumental part in molding – to turn back from the path that he was on.

What had initially started as a somewhat friendly means to gloss over systematic religious abuse poured down from headquarters onto her husband became a battle of attrition that then ended in what sounded like a veiled threat, all before Dr. Phillips exclaimed "GOSH-DARN-IT!" only he didn't use the bywords. He profaned the holy name of the LORD, got up from the booth, dashed over to the counter, paid the total bill, and left for his hotel in some sort of a heated rage. That evening, he'd pull up Todd Driscoll and announce to the congregation how GOD had big plans for this young man. He explained how he and Pastor Jackie had talked at great length and how, while Pastor Jackie would be around – and maybe even there, the stresses and strains of life seemed to be taking a toll on him.

"After all, if we don't take care of our own, how can we help anyone outside of these walls? If we don't help those in the shadow of our steeple, how can we help those across the pond? Charity begins at home, Church. We just need to give Reverend Jackie room to breathe and reflect," he told them.

And while this might have all sounded good on paper, somebody then stood up and asked how long this would go on. Dr. Phillips said perhaps a few weeks, likely a month, then assured everyone that nothing was going on, that Pastor Jackie wasn't leaving or going anywhere, and looked down at his former youth pastor in what seemed like a non-threatening way – but was really to dare him not to say a thing about it.

These congregants didn't need to be pulled into all of this drama. Rev. Todd got up and did a fine job. More than not, he spoke of what an honor it was to work alongside Pastor Jack. After the service ended, Dr. Phillips reminded Jackie again to stay out of the pulpit of that church – his church – until he was told otherwise.

"The men who sent me have their ears to the ground, Brother Jackie. They see and hear everything. Don't think for a moment that just 'cause some of these people are with you that they're with you," Dr. Phillips said.

That would be one of the last things that he would say to him – at a time in his life when he still saw this man as his pastor and friend. Though, even then it hung in some kind of lukewarm Hell.

Penny slipped her arm around her husband and told him – "C'mon, dear. Let's go home."

CHAPTER 08

Behind Closed Doors

Dr. Phillips murmured to himself on his way home. Regret filled his mind that Pastor Jackie Noble had heard him blaspheme the holy name of The LORD like he had. GOD knew that if they were Muslims living out in the desert, instead of Christians the state of Georgia, and he'd used the name of "Allah" as a swearword, he'd likely have his tongue cut out and be left to bleed to death on the spot. Still, The LORD of all creation was patient and kind. He was merciful to forgive and just. Byron felt like after all he'd done for GOD, the man upstairs owed him one; or that's the way that he saw it. Byron Phillips had been in church all of his life and in ministry for what sometimes felt like two lifetimes. He was proud to be a third-generation Pentecostal preacher with his grandaddy receiving the infilling of the Holy Ghost during the Pentecostal resurgence at the turn of the century. His mom and dad were just kids when they married, and thus they had him young. Howbeit, those two were holiness from the top of their heads to the soles of their feet. Thereby, Byron Phillips was raised perpetually teething on a pew. The church was his home and the House of The LORD was home to him. At the church that he went to, his papaw, Reverend Buford Phillips, was the pastor. Buford had lived a hard life and was an Army man. He'd served his time fighting for the freedom of this great country, and everything he did, he

did either GOD's way – as explained in the Holy Bible – or the Army way.

The way that he'd make his bed, polish his shoes, and do just about everything was likened unto an exact science. And while Byron knew that his grandfather loved him, he just wasn't the sort of man to say a thing like that. He'd pray and travail for people at the altar. According to Buford Philips, love could be shown in two ways: suffering and good works. He was a man who put others ahead of himself, ahead of his family, and ahead of most everybody except the LORD Jesus Christ. He was hungry for souls. On his deathbed, he took young Byron by the collar and told him to stay on the straight and narrow.

Byron's father, Rev. Dewey Phillips, wasn't half the preacher that his papaw was – though he'd never tell him that. Buford preached Hellfire and brimstone and nothing but Hellfire and brimstone 24/7, whether people knew about it or not. He'd tell people of the standards of holiness and the weight of sin. He'd tell them that if a person truly received the gift of GOD's grace, they'd put off this world like a snake sheds its skin and thereby grow in Christ. But this wasn't Byron's father. His dad was the seventh of seven sons in a household that had four daughters, and every one of them were the seed of the same man – Buford Phillips – and his wife, Mildred. She lived the kind of life that Papaw Phillips preached women were made for: being fruitful and multiplying. Pretty much every one of those boys – six out of seven – became preachers, just like their daddy. The other, Vernon, who they called Vern, joined up with the military and fought in active combat in the Banana Wars. While over there, he fell in love with a hispanic woman, was disowned by their family, and was forbidden to ever step foot on his daddy's property again. Like their mama

Mildred, the three daughters also married preachers and sustained the continuation of baby-making housewives who were in perfect submission to their husbands, as their husband covered them and he was covered by GOD.

While in ways he was a type and shadow of his father, Rev. Dewey Phillips lacked the fearsome, soul-crushing omniscience that Papaw Phillips held in the eyes of his betrothed. Because of this, every now and then Dewey Phillips felt that it was compulsory to slap his wife around from time to time, just to remind her the pecking order that he preached firmly The LORD had set in Ephesians 8:22-24, which reads:

> "Wives, submit yourselves unto your own husbands, as unto the Lord. For the husband is the head of the wife, even as Christ is the head of the church: and he is the saviour of the body. Therefore as the church is subject unto Christ, so let the wives be to their own husbands in every thing."

Never mind the far harsher prohibitions and heavier burdens that GOD placed on men, whom He called to lead which are in part detailed through the remainder of that chapter and elsewhere. Never mind 1 Peter 3:7 telling a man that if he doesn't honor his wife, it will supernaturally hinder his prayers, and such things. Frankly, if a man even came close to meeting the high mark that GOD Almighty had set for him, any remotely sane woman would want to submit to a man like that. However the failing is when a man doesn't uphold the Bible's standards and yet the hypocritical husband commands his wife to have them imposed on her. It was all so funny to Byron, though not funny haha. He'd heard his daddy, the holiness preacher, use those very words. He'd yell:

"Don't do as I do. Do as I say."

It always struck him some way about the man. Both Dewey and Buford had instilled a little bit of themselves in him. While Dr. Byron Phillips had a far better poker face than most people, behind closed doors he was a far different man than most people might imagine. In the public eye, he was kind and gracious to his wife. Joyce Phillips, on the other hand, always came off as a quiet and mousey person. Once in a local supermarket, a congregant of New Life Fellowship saw the two of them out at the grocery store together on an occasion where she was begging him like a small child for a small container of fresh strawberries. In this somewhat odd occurrence, he deprived her of them, telling his wife that she really didn't need them, then, with a sharp glance, dared her to say anything else about them. To that random parishioner it was merely a fleeting moment in time. To Joyce, it was one of many moments like this stacked upon another and another in her life.

Joyce had lived both a different and disturbingly similar kind of life as her husband, Byron. She was raised in the extremely dry and pious Church of Christ. They had no organ, no piano, and no guitars. While scripture talked about people worshiping The LORD through the playing of musical instruments in the Old Testament, out and out commanded it in some of the Psalms, and prophetically showed that they'd be doing so in the hereafter, for some strange reason this peculiar denomination couldn't put two and two together regarding the matter. And while that may implicate them all as total fools, standing at a far enough distance, one might arguably say: "And what of everyone else?" Certainly, the Pentecostal had standards that, like the application of worshiping through the playing of musical instruments, was endorsed by scripture. An easy one to

point out would be men having facial hair. GOD Almighty, as well as quite literally every man who wasn't a degenerate heathen within the sixty-six canonized books of the Bible, all had beards. At any point in history when the culture turned towards GOD instead of the secular, the men had beards. The enemies of the Jewish people cut off half of the beards of three of King David's ambassadors, and it started a war. Rather than telling them to just trim them evenly, David responded to them how they should not return until their beards had grown out. Frankly, whether the subject of beards or worshiping GOD through the playing of musical instruments, both have so many verses favorable to them that a person could have a ministry where the focal point was on either of those subjects – not that GOD would ever call someone to do such a thing.

Like Byron, Joyce was raised strictly. While she was no preacher's kid, she was the daughter of a cigarette-smoking church deacon who was also an active member of the local Masonic Lodge – both of which wouldn't be permissible within the holiness denomination. Perhaps the only favorable thing to be said of the character of Joyce's father, Dirk – as far as Byron saw it – was that the man was a rampant Georgia Bulldogs fan. For years after marrying her, Byron and Dirk would fight like cats and dogs. They'd argue scripture. They'd argue this thing and that thing also. At its most escalated point, Dirk came peeling into the driveway to drag his little girl back home and get her away from that "crazy, tongue-flapping preacher" – as he disparagingly called him. What erupted from that was a literal knockdown, drag-out fight in the Phillip's gravel driveway. Ever since then, the two of them seemed to have a lot more respect for one another. All of the ugliness more or less stopped. A few times the two of them even went to a few basketball games. The worst thing to happen at any of those was when Dirk introduced Byron to some of his friends from the Masonic Lodge.

"Now this right here is my son-in-law. He's one of them holy-rollers, but I guess none of us can be right about everything," Dirk told them, laughing like it was the funniest joke he'd ever heard himself tell.

Dr. Phillips – who at that time only held a Masters Degree – took Dirk's half-finished Coca Cola and spilled it over his head, right in front of everybody. Strangely, the man just laughed and seemed to like him all the more afterward. While they were different in so many ways, in others,Byron and Dirk were like two peas in a pod. Joyce left home to get away from her father and married a man who was just like him in the way that he treated her and pressed her down. While she knew that he loved her, Byron had some funny ideas about how love worked, and as far as she knew, it was all natural, until she met a widower named Scott who first started attending New Life Fellowship Church in the late 1960s. Ingratiating himself with Dr. Phillips, he became something of his go-fer. He'd go for this and go for that. Somewhere in that time, he became a trusted friend of Sister Joyce, and while nothing sexual ever happened between the two of them, she had the worst kind of affair that a woman could have: an emotional one.

Despite the fact that it didn't go far physically – no more than a loving embrace or him supportively holding her hand – Dr. Byron Phillips reviled the man, excommunicated him from the church, and inwardly even felt that affliction, which the doctors diagnosed as Lou Gehrig's Disease, was the judgment of GOD for her transgressions against him. They'd slept in separate bedrooms from that time onward. Dr. Phillips had passed

by her room and such, looking down upon her, telling her to look at what she'd brought upon herself. In his mind, it seemed that his prayers for vindication had been partially answered, and yet as far as he could tell, nothing had befallen the kindhearted widower named Scott. After all of that, the thought of touching her in the way that husbands touch their wives did not appeal to him. More and more, he convinced himself that just like men in the Old Testament had concubines and it was all well enough in the sight of The LORD – so would he. The young lady that he had chosen to fulfill this role was her nursemaid. Her name was Carol Robinson.

Even before all of this had happened, Carol was a member of their church. She was always so helpful to Pastor Byron. She wasn't bad looking. She was enamored with him and was somewhat slow-witted. He knew all of the things to say, all of the scriptures to twist. Really, in ways, it was no wonder that he'd advocated for protecting Pastor Russell Ledbetter – though he found his deeds distasteful and most foul. All the while, his own misdoings he justified. Yessir, in the great balance of things, Byron Phillips assured himself how he'd come a long way from his daddy. He never put the leather of his belt to her back and other places where the bruises wouldn't show. Most of what he did to submit her was with words. Nobody would ever see the deep cuts they caused. Of course, he felt right in doing it because if she hadn't been acting some way, he wouldn't have said the things that he did when nobody was around to hear them. As though trying to kill a housefly with a 12-gauge shotgun, he'd come down on Joyce like the wrath of GOD, feeling proud of himself for keeping her humble. It was all because of this that a hidden part of her longed for the soft touch of a man and gentle, loving embrace from someone who wouldn't hurt her the way that every man who was closest to her had. Byron expected as

much, though he'd never think about it quite the same way as she would. He suspected that a part of her loved their excommunicated church member, Scott, in a way that she could never love him. Byron had ranted and raved so many times to her how that man was going straight to Hell and then at some point felt so broken and unfulfilled by her that he coaxed Carol Robinson into his bed.

There that first time and every other time – sometimes two and three times in a row for weeks – he'd go off with her into the other room while his wife was bedfast, unable to do anything. The squeaking of springs, pounding of the bed frame, and guttural moans that the two made from the pastor's bedroom told her the story of what was going on. When this was not happening and she was alone with Byron, something deep down inside of him would fester up and damn her, explaining that she brought this ailment on herself when she tied herself to Scott. Further, he'd emphasize that she brought all of this on herself. Joyce would cry during her pastor husband's throes of lustful passion with her nursemaid – as well as at other times. Both this and periodic spurts of laughter were part of the condition. A man with all of the misconception that he had would never think that the chronic abuse that she had suffered along with other outside factors might open a door in the multi-chambered housing of her soul for something malevolent to come inside of her. How odd it is that the things people blame GOD for are brought about by mankind and the Devil?

Her only comfort was that she genuinely loved the LORD. She did not understand any of this, for she had no one to teach her. She could not get free from these chains, for there was no one with the faith, insight, teaching, love, and compassion to break her chains.

There had only ever been two men who had shown her nothing but kindness. One was a friend whom her jealous and controlling husband cast out of church; the other died on a cross for her two thousand years ago. When she found the words to speak, she'd typically sing under her breath, which sounded like a muttering, mumbling rhythm.

"I'm saved and I know that I am,
I'm saved and I know that I am,
I'm saved and I know that I am,
I'm so glad I know that I am!"

—were usually the words that one would hear before dissolving into the Hellish nothingness that consumed her world. Either tears would flow or laughter would sound. Either way, her songs of thanksgiving and praise to the GOD in Heaven would be quenched. Inwardly, her only solace was in knowing that this was the only Hell that she'd ever see and that Heaven was a good place filled with good people like Scott who'd never hurt her like her father and husband had.

It was very late when the Rev. Dr. Byron Phillips finally pulled into his driveway and walked through the front door of his home. All the same, a lamp was on, as his wife's nursemaid and his paramour sat in the den, reading her Bible, while she waited for him to return. The poor dim-minded woman had had her thoughts molded in a certain sort of way that was convenient for the pastor. He was a man above reproach who'd just returned from the unfortunate task of taking disciplinary action against a just man. Joyce had been tucked into bed for hours. After getting a drink of water, Byron stripped down to his undershorts and slid into his bed where Carol was waiting. She kissed and nuzzled him in a way that might be regarded as provocative and

endearing, but after he expressed how exhausted he was, like he felt that any good woman should, she put his needs ahead of hers turned over onto her side so that he might spoon her and drift off to sleep.

Far away from all of this, the Reverend Jackie Noble tossed and turned, reliving the utter nightmare of what was happening to him at the very hands of ministers who held elected offices – who'd pledged themselves to do the will of The LORD. The forces of darkness ravaged his world. The only consolation to Jackie was in knowing that if he wasn't doing something right – the Devil wouldn't be fighting him so hard. He'd wake up several times with tears running down his face. He'd pray, asking GOD to judge his heart, and if there be any unclean thing in him to purge it from him as with hyssop. While darkness had come to his world, he knew the darker everything was around you – the brighter your light would seem to shine for all the world to see.

CHAPTER 19
Pressed Down

Finally, having gone back to sleep for what had been the dozenth time or so, nearly an hour and a half before he had to awaken, Jackie Noble was stirred by the sound of the coffee pot singing his song. Monday, September 25th, 1972, had come. Back in his years in college, there was a popular television show that some of the guys and girls used to watch – airing from 1959-1974. A particular fellow named Barry used to quote the introduction of it regularly, in fact, so regularly that it stuck in Jackie's head and was playing in it now. He began to recite the opening narration like a soliloquy as he walked into the kitchen to greet his wife.

> "'You're traveling through another dimension, a dimension not only of sight and sound but of mind. A journey into a wondrous land whose boundaries are that of imagination. That's the signpost up ahead – your next stop, the Twilight Zone,'" he said.
>
> "I remember hearing about that show from some of the girls I used to go to college with. I bet things must sure feel that way to you now, huh?" Penny answered.
>
> "It's just like the man that I've known for all of these years as a pastor and friend has been taken over by someone else. It's just like all of these men that I've admired for so long have

become other people altogether," Jackie responded.

Pouring him a cup of his beloved Maxwell House instant coffee, she remarked as to the possibility that perhaps neither of them really knew who any of these people truly were. He took a sip as though to calm his nerves in a way that little else but the delicious caffeinated beverage would and answered as to how it really broke his heart. Then, something they had talked about and would be brought up again was how Dr. Phillips exclaimed a blasphemy in anger. They both were shocked to hear that out of the mouth of a man of GOD. There were even some pure sinners that they knew who might say all manner of ungodliness, but using the name of Jesus Christ or GOD The Father in some sort of a profane manner was something they had too much character, class, and teaching to do.

Quite frankly, the miraculous workings of The LORD as ministered through Rev. Jackie Noble had seemed to have brought little more than pain. Always trying to be an encouragement, Penny did point out as to how all of this seemed so much like the way the church of Christ's day treated Him for healing someone. And while the parallels were evident, and he knew it to be true, this fatal blow had thus far come to him by only those people who, in one way or another, were close enough to stick the knife in. It'd not come from the Methodists down the street. He was physically losing congregants at his church and, now, maybe even his church entirely. It left him to wonder where GOD was in all of this. And still, he knew that the thing we were all called to was faithfulness. Thus, all there seemed to do was to trust and obey.

Jackie thanked The LORD for the breakfast and asked him to bless the hands that prepared it before he began to eat. Looking up at his dear Penny, he was reminded as to how good he had it. She was a true companion and friend. It was his personal feeling that GOD put her into his life as a reminder of how much He loved him. They spoke sweet nothings to each other as he expressed his thanks for her for always being everything that he needed her to be. Penny likewise told Jackie how proud she was of the man of GOD that she married. Whether the high-ups at church headquarters recognized him or not – she knew who the man that she married was, and GOD did too.

Inwardly, both of them hoped that this whole thing would all blow over soon. In a week or two, Bishop Russell Ledbetter would be removed from his pastoral position at a church of five thousand people – required church disciplinary action – and attend mandatory church counseling, and Pastor Jackie Noble would be reinstated, thanked for his long-suffering sincerity, and apologized to. And rightfully so; it is what should have happened already. Still, wanting and knowing never necessarily changed anything. Jackie Noble got himself ready, turned the key of his 1968 Chevrolet station wagon, backed out of the driveway onto the road, put it in gear, and drove off to work.

He played his glorious Southern gospel music all the way there. Like David playing his harp soothed King Saul's soul in scripture, the sweet, worshipful sounds of GOD's kind of music brought momentary peace for him. Jackie wasn't the first to feel that way, either, and he wouldn't be the last. Just a year before, the fiery Assemblies of GOD pastor and worldwide evangelist Rev. Jimmy Swaggart began his television ministry. The minister's music played across the gospel stations, and

his preaching played across radio. He, too, loved Southern gospel and had even emphatically stated that if it's not Southern gospel – it's not gospel – as a jab against the new sort of rock-'n'-Roll-infused Jesus people music that was playing across the airways from the California hills and alike.

It would be a long day for Jackie Noble, for the reason of some people politely asking him how the big camp meeting went that he was always so joyful about, as well as others – who knew he'd be getting a big break preaching at it – asking how that went. He just wished that he'd have a good answer for them. He just wished he'd have a good answer for anybody. It was a day to be filled with questions, questions, and more questions – on a very on-and-off basis. Outside of the six to seven people at his work who thought it might be nice to talk about it with him – there was still that reporter, who'd come to see him from afar off, at church. Like shattered glass, the miraculous was leaving an immensity of fallout. Most of it was around the area where it hit and just like a broken glass, some pieces somehow managed to make their way halfway across the house. Just when you thought you'd got them all – there'd be another.
At a distance, though, it couldn't really hurt him. Jackie thought that it must be more like a freak show or some kind of oddity. To them, he must have been the kind of thing found in circuses and fairs.

"Come one, come all, to see the fabulous exorcist, Jackie Noble. He's cast out demons from blackest Africa, the orient, and places so dark and scary that no explorer has ever gone," they'd say in his mind.

Surely, he was nothing more to these people than the tattooed man or bearded lady. Yet, this perhaps was the only audience he had to preach to through the papers, rag-papers, or whatever sort of magazine it might be. When he met the fellow, the man was more than kind. He took him out to lunch and wanted to know everything. He was also informative enough to tell Jackie about some of the other papers that would run his story. He encouragingly said that they were all respectful, and it just seemed like a miraculous story of faith, hope, and encouragement for people to read about – and how they might let GOD in their lives, somehow, through it. Like a sleazy used car salesman this guy really knew the right words to say to get someone to spill. He wanted to know it all, the full scoop, the whole scoop, and nothing less.

With a sincere face and honest smile, the reporter – whose name was Max – began to converse back and forth, taking notes about everything. He was completely enthralled with the whole thing and even offered to stay another day and do this tomorrow, adding how he was sure that his editor would let him for a story like this. Much to Jackie's surprise, that was exactly what happened. It was during these encounters that the man told Jackie how – due to some of the press stories being out in the papers – one reporter from an independent Atlanta rag slipped into the camp meeting service just to check him out and wrote an article on that.

If nothing else, the affair at the time was cathartic. It in some way gave Jackie Noble an outlet to minister by the power of his testimony as to the mighty works that the hand of The LORD had done through him. Max had his phone number and address, as well as enough information on the church organization that Jackie held license through to send some complimentary copies to headquarters if he so chose. Outside of this, the whole week was something of a down note. He was a pastor who, for a time, was no longer pastoring – at no real fault of his own. Each week that subsequently went by bore the same grim sadness. In the sermons that Rev. Todd Driscoll preached, as well as the Sunday School lessons that Brother Tony Edwards taught, he'd see himself.

"'He is despised and rejected of men; a man of sorrows, and acquainted with grief: and we hid as it were our faces from him; he was despised, and we esteemed him not,'" Rev. Driscoll would say – and Jackie would think about how Christ, too, had been persecuted rejected by church people, all for doing the perfect will of GOD The Father through the power of the Holy Ghost.

He'd see himself in Jeremiah and in Ezekiel. He'd see himself in Job, sitting there amidst his so-called comforter. Rev. Todd Driscoll would fill in for Jackie Noble as the interim pastoral speaker for three consecutive weeks, from the Sundays of October 1st - 15th. On Wednesday Evening, the 18th, he'd make an announcement that headquarters had contacted him on Tuesday, as for a little while, Souls Harbor Holiness Church was to have the pleasure of hosting the evangelistic speaker Rev. Ike Watkins. Now, Ike was a fireball from not too many miles away. Despite this, he seemed like he stayed out of the area more than in it. He and Rev. Harold Sizemore had even preached evangelistic crusades together, and while Ike Watkins wasn't at the same caliber on the sociopolitical scale as Brother Sizemore, he too seemed to have a revivalistic atmosphere that followed him.

The Watkins family had seven children, many of whom they'd adopted. Interestingly enough – each of them played a musical instrument. Ike played, his wife played, the children played, and they all sang. Several of the young boys had begun preaching as well and were being groomed into something of the sort by their father to enter into successful evangelistic careers. While Ike and his family certainly lived close enough to have regularly attended Souls Harbor Holiness Church, they always tended to go the other way. It was something that Jackie and Penny Noble had been thankful for as Ike and his wife were known among some preachers to have a takeover spirit – and they made it feel natural. Jackie Noble – who'd been commanded to sit on his hands while his faithful colaborer spoke in his stead, was now being subjected to headquarters letting a fox in his hen house. On that Thursday evening after work, Jackie called Dr. Phillips to have a word with him about it. Dr. Phillips passed the whole thing off as something that they'd just be doing for a few weeks – and furthermore, suggested that Jackie calm down. Besides all of that, he apologized for how poorly things had gone between the two of them, assuring Jackie how he'd always been his friend. He asked him to come up to West Point for a visit on Saturday, October 28th, so the two of them could get together and talk.

> "I'm still on your side, Jackie boy. I've always been on your side, and that isn't about to change," he told him.

All that he spoke were smooth and kind words. They were seemingly the words that would be spoken by any true friend, or extraordinarily crafty devil. While the thought never occurred to him that this must have been the way that Joab spoke to Abner, before he neighborly put his arm around him and pierced the general of Saul beneath his fifth rib – it most certainly may have been. Still, whatever thing lay before him was uncertain. The words were that of a friend, thus indicating that it either was that or a devil masquerading itself as an angel of light. Ike Watkins preached and fire fell from Heaven. As expected, he and his family took complete control of the service. Just like a vampire bat's fangs are so sharp that an animal can't feel them slide in, so was he just as sharp.

In the most natural of ways, he was complementary – even flattering – towards Sister Eleanor and Martha as his family joined together overtaking the music. And while music is often regarded as subjective in taste and style, no remotely sane person would have been able to see any of this as anything but an overwhelming improvement. With the quality of Elvis Presley, The Mamas and The Papas, or any other legitimate rock-''-roll band of whom Jackie, Penny, and the overwhelming majority of their church hadn't heard – with the exclusion of Elvis' gospel songs – the Watkins family raised the bar of what Sunday Morning worship ought to look and sound like. Riding right along beside this, his sermon matched.

Rev Ike Watkins preached on being facilitators of revival, about a spirit of revival, and about bringing revival. It was revival this and revival that. He'd tell people dramatic things like how they didn't want true revivals, how they couldn't handle real revival, and how if their hearts weren't set, revival could be happening all around them and they miss it. The way that he said it, too, was in a sense brilliant. It neither came on as pious, nor as condemning. It sounded more like a double-dog-dare. Ike and his family would be there for every consecutive service until Jackie met up with Dr. Phillips on Saturday the 28th. Besides that, they were

announced to be there the week after, also. Everything else seemed unknown, and while the people loved Jackie's preaching – they loved this, too. Really, who could blame them? Inwardly, Jackie and Penny wondered if the leadership at Headquarters was trying to put them out and the Watkins in. Were they trying to turn their hearts towards another, or was this some kind of subtle threat? It was cause for concern, and unanswered questions always seem to cause speculation.

Jackie had been told each and every time that headquarters was praying about what to do, and he'd been given no expectation that they'd let him know anything by any kind of deadline at all. "I'll pray about it" had probably been a preachy put-off for hundreds of years, Jackie thought, though there were some that meant it. The general council's time in prayer did seem less sincere when he found out – the week of Sunday, October 22nd – that Bishop Russell Ledbetter had been talked with by the general council. That he offered a private apology to them, and had been reinstated as the pastor of his church, with little more than a slap on the wrist on that Sunday – and him only taking a leave for four of those weeks. He'd also heard that during the time of his suspension, Pastor Ledbetter had gone on some sort of extravagant vacation getaway to calm his nerves. He and Jackie were two different breeds of preacher indeed.

While Jackie Noble had been suffering – in a perpetual status of one in sackcloth and ashes – Russell Ledbetter had been living it up as though he didn't have a care in the world. Frankly, it wouldn't surprise Jackie if he was writing another book. He'd already put out one about tithing, gaining wealth, and such things. It was a big-time seller for him, too. The only real encouragement that Jackie got – if you could call it that – was from the secular newspapers, that people would mail to his home, that testified of his casting-out demons in rural Georgia.

They rolled in sporadically. Some days there'd be one, others there'd be two or three, but most often, there'd be nothing. The temper and tone varied from paper to paper. At worst, it was viewed with criticism and disbelief at best, it was asked if he'd be the next Jimmy Swaggart, Billy Graham, or what have you. It was already a rough year for the church. While GOD was doing great things, the devil was fighting back hard. In the month of July, a religious – or rather, sacrilegious – documentary came out called *Marjoe*. It was filmed the year prior – 1971 – and followed the former child preacher evangelist, Marjoe Gortner, who sought to disgrace the church by showing what a fake preacher he and others had been for years. The man was a true showman and made it clear that he now sought to leave the church world behind him and run towards the Hollywood lights rather than the Light of this World – Jesus Christ. While the Reverend Billy Graham was packing out stadiums, leading people to Christ by the power of the Holy Ghost, the fallen Pentecostal evangelist, Marjoe, sought to lead them away through the power of cinema with the soon-to-be award-winning documentary that bore his name.

In the midst of all of this, Saturday – October 28th, 1972 – had finally come. Jackie drove to West Point, Alabama alone. As he traveled the road, he began to reflect to himself not just merely about the weeks that preceded all of this, but the good times as well. After all, he'd known Dr. Phillips for a long time. When Jackie started going there, they'd even had a baby. It would be Byron and Joyce's only child. The baby was a boy who was named Buford – after his grandfather – howbeit, this child's life only lasted two years in this world. The baby was a water-head. Dr. Phillips and his wife seemed to

love their son so. They'd have big prayer services, hoping for his healing. They'd call for fasts so that the church might believe, together, that Christ would restore their son to perfect health. He only received that healing in the great beyond, as the angels carried him away to rest in the arms of Jesus. Jackie and Penny were both there at the child's funeral. They'd rejoiced with the family in their good times and grieved with them at times like that. Shortly thereafter, Byron and Joyce decided never to have any more children. She, rather than her husband, went to the hospital to get an operation that would prevent her from ever getting pregnant again. In some minor conversation which only now seemed to be resonating like it had not before, Jackie remembered a short little nothing when Dr. Phillips explained away why he didn't get an operation instead – using the Mosaic Law, the priesthood, and prohibition against one having crushed testicles not being able to enter into the house of The LORD – as his justification. He'd also said that Joyce just couldn't have good babies, deferring the child's abnormality to his mother alone, and then quickly stopped as though catching himself. Jackie thought at that time how his pastor and mentor was so grieved that he could hardly be held accountable for anything he had said. And so, onward he drove, taking a trip through corridors of vaulted memories all the way there.

Besides everything else, he thought of all of the good times. He remembered how kind Dr. Phillips had always been to himself and Penny, as well as countless others. There was no doubt as to why he had always regarded the man so highly. Their appointment together was even going to be a bit more intimate, as it was at his home. While Jackie had offered that he could bring Penny to see and pray with Joyce, Dr. Phillips rejected that offer in the most polite of ways. He told Jackie how her health was really so poor.

"She's an afflicted woman, stricken down with this godless disease, just like our boy was years ago. We're just trying to make the best of it that we can. She has a nurse, Carol, who is here at the house more than not. That woman is a godsend. I really just don't know how I'd handle everything without her," he'd told him.

Finally, around lunch time, Jackie arrived at the Phillips' home. It had been years since the two of them had been together there, and while they'd had some recent encounters that weren't so great, all of the pleasantries of the man he once knew– or thought that he knew – came flooding back to his mind.

Jackie parked his station wagon, and got out, only to have Dr. Phillips meet him at the door.
"It's good to get together with you, Jack," he told him in a sobering tone, placing one hand firmly on his shoulder and giving him what could best be described as a fatherly smile.

"It's good to be here with you, too," Jackie replied, more out of a sense of cordiality and sentiment to what they'd had for so long than his immediate feelings in the present.

With that, Dr. Phillips invited him in. The hushed voice of Carol Robinson came from the kitchen, explaining to Joyce that Jackie was there and how she'd just be away for a moment to say hello. After this, she walked into the living room, where the two men had sat down and asked if she could get them a glass of water, some coffee, or something.

"You drink coffee?" Jackie asked his pastor.

"I know a lot of people frown on it, but yes – I do. I'd actually heard word that you like the caffeinated devil, too," Dr. Phillips answered jestingly.

Both of them told Carol that they'd love a cup. Likewise, both of them took theirs black. She remarked how the two of them were making her job easy, heard Mrs. Phillips crying – to which she called out that she'd be with her in a minute – and went off into the kitchen to pour both of them a cup.

"Is she…" Jackie asked in regards to Mrs. Phillips, but before he could finish his sentence, Dr. Phillips interjected.

"She hasn't been all right for years. I feel like Job. First, I lose a son after two insufferable years of going in and out of the doctor, prayer meetings, and corporate fasting. Now, this. It's her condition. Sometimes she laughs. Sometimes she cries. Her mobility and speech are affected. It's just like some sort of living Hell for all of us. Thank GOD that we have Carol around. Sometimes I begin to feel like she's the only one around here helping me to stay sane, you know."

"I can't even begin to imagine," Jackie answered him with genuine compassion and care.

Little more than this was said before Carol reentered the room with two steaming cups of black coffee. Smiling, she asked Dr. Phillips how his was, as he had sipped it almost immediately in anticipation of the question.

"Good to the last drop," he answered with a grin, immediately prompting Jackie to taste.

"Well, isn't that something? You and I have the same brand," he told him.

"Great minds think alike," Dr. Phillip retorted back.

Just for a moment, before getting down to business, he was back there again in that room with the friend who he'd always loved and thought so highly of. Meanwhile, back home, Penny was answering phone calls from church folks asking if they were leaving the church. Their questions brought up all sorts of conversations. Jackie's probation had raised more than a few eyebrows, leaving folks to wonder what was going on. The most hurt of any of them were the young people, who'd regularly engage Pastor Jackie after service, asking him what was going on. He'd pass it off that they were just trying to let some other guys adhere to their calling – and such evasive answers as that – without telling people the whole truth.

And with that said, there were people who knew the truth or enough of it. Various leaks from what had happened at their annual holiness camp meeting began to spread some of the church like wildfire. Penny knew that she and her husband would have to be back in the saddle soon to bring about peace, or the collateral damage on souls would start taking effect – if it hadn't already – and she knew that it had. Some church folks were already going up to Rev. Watkins and asking him questions.

"Can a Christian have a demon?" one of the dissenters would say.

And of course, going off of what Papaw said instead of sound Biblical doctrine, Ike would wrongly answer them, "No."

Most people had no idea about these sorts of things. They'd never been put in a place where they were pressured to do so. And if they were, they'd just tend to make it up as they went along. Once, at a meeting, Rev. Harold Sizemore told everyone in the general vicinity to cover their ears and hold their noses so they wouldn't become possessed by the demon he was about to cast out of some young person – who'd just started going to a church where the Rev. spoke. It was a story that he told time and time again. He said that the exorcism went on for about three hours. At some point, a kid slipped out of the church, walked to the end of the block, called for an ambulance, and they eventually came and hauled the kid away. These people weren't living in the same world as Pastor Jackie was. Just like how the enemy sows the tares among the wheat and they grow up together, not everything that goes on in church is as real as everything else.

Dr. Phillips and Jackie's conversation was going well enough in some regards and horribly in others. While the general council seemed to feel like they held some sovereign omniscience about decisions they rendered – and thereby would not apologize for how poorly they'd treated him – he did plan to let him retake his pulpit on Sunday, November 5th. As for tomorrow, Rev. Ike Watkins and his family would be there for their last intermedial service at Souls Harbor Holiness Church before heading back out on the evangelistic trail. Jackie could just hear Ike Watkins now politely thanking him for the opportunity, prophesying blessings over him, his wife, and the church, saying all of the usual things that he says, and being on their way.

Before heading home, though, Jackie did think how it'd be good to pray with Sister Joyce. As it would so happen, Carol pushed her wheelchair into the living room, and Jackie abruptly interrupted his and Dr. Phillips' conversation in order to call out to her.

"Hey, Sister Joyce. It's Jackie. Do you remember me?" he asked her, quickly rising to his feet and moving nearer to the infirm woman.

She was hardly responsive, but whatever measure in which she did respond, it was so garbled up that a person had to use their imagination to insert an answer over the incoherent mumble.

"I love you, Honey. It's been such a long time. It's so nice to see you again. Would you like for me to pray for you?" he said.

She had been looking up at him, wooden faced, with some sort of something in her eyes like you might imagine on a wounded animal. Then, she began crying.

"Lord, Father, I pray that you'd touch my sister. Lord, we know that you are the great healer and you alone have the power to do what the doctors cannot do. Touch this sickness," he called out – her crying turned to coughing like she was trying to get something loose – and then when he began to speak, over this sickness, she started to laugh.

"All of this… all of this is part of her condition. My word. She's been this way for so long, Jack. The doctors have tried to help her. You know how it is. It's in The LORD's hands," Dr. Phillips interrupted, coming in on some of the last of that prayer.

Jackie ended with asking GOD to touch her and then said – "In the name of Jesus, amen." At which point she let out a blood-curdling cry as though she'd been stabbed. Dr. Phillips leapt up and barked out at Carol to take Mrs. Phillips to her room. It all seemed a bit much to him. More than that, he quenched what was happening.

Dr. Phillips halfway composed himself, telling Jackie how he didn't know why GOD let things happen like this to some people and not others – though in his thinking, this was the handiwork of The LORD for the emotional affair she'd had on him – and how he'd feel so very validated if that man – Scott – lay dead in a gin-soaked gutter somewhere. Wiping his head, Dr. Phillips then insisted that whereas Jackie had come out all of that way, he wanted to do something nice for him for lunch. It was at this time when Carol questioned, wouldn't they rather have something there, but he brushed her off and said that whereas Mrs. Phillips seemed to be acting particularly stirred up, it would seem best to him if they'd both leave. From the cracked door of her bedroom the poor woman so helpless looked out towards Jackie Noble as if she wanted to cry out for him to save her. Momentarily, he looked deep into her – but before anything else could come of it, Dr. Byron Phillips took Jackie by the arm and told him how he'd love the place where he was taking him.

As they passed out of sight, he almost could swear that he saw a slight smile come across her face like a cat has when it's playing with its food. As the two of them walked out the door, they heard more garbled laughter rumbling from out of her.

"It's her affliction that causes this. Whatever has gotten into her has made her this way. She's either laughing or crying. She's become so infirmed. But when we wed, we vowed unto The LORD, for better or worse. It seems that I just got the 'worse' part," Dr. Phillips told him.

On Sunday, October 29th, 1972, Reverend Ike Watkins would preach his final sermon during Pastor Jackie Noble's suspension. Just as Jackie had imagined, he spoke all of the well wishes and blessings over him that were typical. In the purest of King James English and prophetic tones, he'd exclaim, "Thus saith The LORD" this, and "Thus saith The LORD" that, then they'd be on their way. On the following Monday, he'd come home to Penny, who had a note that she wrote down of some ministry that was wanting Jackie to call them back. It was something about preaching at a conference. They ate dinner; he called and encouragingly talked, agreeing to speak at some kind of gospel crusade meeting, that December, put on by some folks who'd read about him in the paper.

On their way down to the supermarket that evening, he told his wife the whole story. One of the men whom they had scheduled was now unable to make it and they wanted him instead. And oddly enough, these people knew about all of the supernatural occurrences and weren't put off by them, but rather drawn to them instead.

"It sounds like GOD is really putting something together," Penny told Jackie encouragingly.

"Dear, I've seen it time and time again all through life. GOD is always faithful – it's men who aren't," he answered her with a humble look of solemnity and thanksgiving for all The LORD had done, was doing, and would do.

CHAPTER 10

Shaken Together

Awakening that Tuesday, October 31st, 1972, Jackie surveyed coworkers, parents, and their children playing dress up and pretending to be something other than what they were for the commercialized pagan holiday of Halloween. While many of them likely didn't know it's dark origins involving the sacrificing of children to the frightful druidic gods, where they'd melt down their fat to make candles, cutting out faces in gourds where they'd place the candle in and call it the jack-of-the-lantern, along with other semblances involving knocking on doors and candy in commemoration of Samhain – nor did they know that in Central America, their nearly necromantic rituals regarded people seeking to reunite with and/or appease the dead, the creation of sweets called sugar skulls as an pagan offerings in commemoration All Hallows Eve – the reverend knew its demonic origins all too well. Still, them playing dress-up did bring his mind back to the far more heinous thing of some of his fellow clergymen wearing masks every day of the year – pretending to be something that they were not – and then others not taking something that is deadly serious, serious at all once they're found in their sin; of the two, this was the far heavier matter. And thus, there he watched the people walking about dressed as devils and angels, saints and sinners, ravenous beasts and law givers with the larger issue being who they really were on the inside. Did they really walk with Christ or was their going to church just a matter of dress-up? One day, the judge of the Universe, who weighs all things and sees all things, would separate the wheat from the chaff. As scripture says:

> "For if we sin wilfully after that we have received the knowledge of the truth, there remaineth no more sacrifice for sins, But a certain fearful looking for of judgment and fiery indignation, which shall devour the adversaries. He that despised Moses' law died without mercy under two or three witnesses: Of how much sorer punishment, suppose ye, shall he be thought worthy, who hath trodden under foot the Son of God, and hath counted the blood of the covenant, wherewith he was sanctified, an unholy thing, and hath done despite unto the Spirit of grace? For we know him that hath said, Vengeance belongeth unto me, I will recompense, saith the Lord. And again, The Lord shall judge his people. It is a fearful thing to fall into the hands of the living God."

> – HEBREWS 10:26-31

As these thoughts sojourned through Jackie's head, a coworker named Jeremy tapped his shoulder. As just looking around, he saw the man dressed in a bright red hooded cap with horns atop his head, as well a bright red jumpsuit that had a long, somewhat phallic tail – as the fabric spear portion of its edges were rounded and dulled. In his hand, he also held a red plastic trident.

"I've been praying for you, brother. I hope things get better soon," he said.

Jackie smiled, thanking Ryan and telling him that he'd be back up in the pulpit this coming Sunday. Likewise, he told him about the gospel crusade he'd be preaching at on Saturday, December 9th in the state of Florida. While he couldn't rightly remember the name of it at the time, it had a beach in it, or was near the beach, or something like that. And while Jackie and Penny Noble weren't beach-going people – as they saw all of this as place of lust and all holiness people disparagingly called coed swimming: mixed-bathing – still, if The LORD wanted to do a mighty thing at the beach, Rev. Jackie Noble was all in. After all, he proposed – if there was ever going to be a baptizing, the water was already there.

While the Nobles in no way meant to glorify the unholy celebration of Halloween, they did try to take full advantage of the fact that lost, broken people in need of a savior would be coming to their door. It was because of this that each year, Penny would make brownies, cookies, and other sorts of homemade goodies to feed their bodies – likewise, while ministering to the physical, the Nobles would hand out small New Testaments that they got from the Gideon's to feed their souls. And while after doing this, they'd generally wish them a "Happy Halloween" as a commercialized kindness that sat well with most, they'd also sanctify it by tacking on a Jesus loves you at the end.

After all of this would come Wednesday, Pastor Jackie's first night back in the pulpit of the church he'd loved and labored for so very hard. As he approached the pulpit it, became clear to everyone that he had not lost a bit of his resolve. His message that evening – if it

was a message as much as it was a testimony – came from Psalm 121; and while there were eight verses in total, his focus was on the first two.

> "'I will lift up mine eyes unto the hills, from whence cometh my help. My help cometh from the LORD, which made heaven and earth."
>
> – PSALM 121:1b-2

From thence, he expounded as to how in near-eastern pagan culture, as well many pagan cultures, the divine was said to dwell on mountaintops and other such high places that were unattainable to man. That is why they'd build ziggurats and put their pagan shrines on high mountains and hills – so that they would be closer in proximity and their god would come meet them at that place on their terms rather than them coming to the one true GOD on His terms, in his way. What David was saying as he looked out at the faulty ways of men is that he saw all of these vain things, and in defiance of the demonic, asked where did his help come from – much as the Prophet Elisha cried out, "Where is the LORD GOD of Elijah" before parting the Jordan river and walking across of dry ground. And like Elisha – who smote the water with his ascended teacher's prayer shawl, David, too, answered his own question in saying that he knew that his help came from The LORD, the maker of heaven and earth.

> "I'm here to tell you, friend, that there are people who put their hope on other men – who'll let them down. There are people who put their confidence in their workplace, only for the doors to close. There are people who put their confidence in their own strength, only for it to fail them, too. But, the race isn't given to the swift, nor is the battle given to the strong, or bread to the

wise, or riches to men of understanding, nor favor to men of skill! Let me tell you something now – this world will fail you. I know there has been some talk going on. People have been wondering why this organization sat Pastor Jackie Noble down. Well, Honey, I've been going back and forth within myself whether I should say it or not – and I guess I'd better just go ahead and say it.

The LORD GOD Almighty opened the door for me to preach on Friday morning at camp meeting, but He didn't just have me preach to give a word. He just didn't have me get up there to knock the devil out of some little girl. The LORD got me up there to expose some bigger devils than I even knew were out there. It breaks my heart, Church. There are preachers out there preaching for money. There are pastors out there playing games. With GOD as my witness, I've never asked for one dime from any of you people. I sell shoes for commission at J. C. Penny! But I'll tell you something else, if this church got to a place where I couldn't do both, where I was blessed enough to receive a salary – like the Levitical priests of old – I'd feel like I'd have to earn it!

Now that's not to say that GOD called anybody to please a cigarette-sucking deacon board like the Baptists do. My word! If GOD wanted anybody to smoke like that, they'd have a chimney coming out of their head! Let me tell you another thing, Church – The LORD didn't call you to please some Cardinal or Bishop or the Pope – like the Catholics do. Jesus Christ is our authority! Jesus Christ is our High Priest! We're living in a day when all kinds of questions are arising, but the answer is still the same, no matter what anyone wants to believe. His name is Jesus Christ.

Let me tell you something, Church: on that final day, it's not gonna matter what everybody else thinks of you – it's only going to matter what GOD thinks of you. If you're just giving Him 99% of your life, then you're in rebellion. Stop playing games with sin! Come out from among the world and be a peculiar people! Can I get a witness?" he cried with fervency.

Beads of sweat trickled down the pastor's forehead as tears ran down his face. People began to praise The LORD and holler. Some young people came to the altar and received Jesus Christ into their hearts, but it was only just getting started. Yessir, that night they had a knock-down, drag-out, barn-burner of a service. If a person could shout the paint off of the walls or shout the grass off the side of a hill, this church would have. While there were some preachers who equate success with how many butts they had planted in seats, Jackie Noble was more concerned with how many of them were going to Heaven. Real revival, after all, isn't how high you can jump, or how you shout – but how you walk when you're ten feet outside the church-house door. If there is no change on the inside, carrying through to the outside, then there is no revival.

Now that he was back in action, Pastor Jackie Noble was back with a vengeance. As far as he was concerned he might as well have been the one that GOD had chosen to get that whole county saved, sanctified, and filled with the Holy Ghost – with the evidence of speaking in tongues. Not missing a beat, he took some plays out of the fiery evangelist Ike Watkins' playbook and demanded that the people let GOD know whether they really wanted revival or not. He began to assemble a call to prayer. Various hours throughout the day, they'd have anyone who signed up to pray, praying. Whereas they wanted to be sure to be thorough, this call a to twenty-four-hours, seven-days-a-week prayer wasn't just limited to one person doing it during those times, nor just to the members of their church.

"I want all y'all to spread the word. Have people contact Sister Penny. She's marking it down. She's taking names. By the grace of GOD, I'm gonna drive my foot so far up Satan's hind-end that it'll take the jaws of life to remove it! I'm tired of the enemy coming in and stealing the joy that GOD had for you and for your children. I'm tired of those devils coming in trying to spoil your harvest.

Church did you know that the enemies' attacks on you aren't about what you have done, but about who they can see that you're going to be in The LORD, unless they can stop you first? I'm telling you – don't let them! I'm telling you right here – right now – fight back! Greater is He that is in me – greater is He that is in this church – greater is He that is in you than he that is in the world," Pastor Jackie boldly exclaimed, but he didn't just say it that once. This call to prayer was broadcast during each and every service at the beginning and the end.

Pastor Jackie Noble would tell the people how a Christian church without discipleship was a Christian church without Christ. He'd tell the people how they were all called to go out into the highways and the byways and lead others to the LORD. The Apostle Paul offered a grave condemnation in scripture for so-called Christians who'd sat derelict in their faith – or lack thereof – never having transitioned from the simplicity of the milk of the Word to the meat of the Word. He explained how if a person was going to church for themselves alone, then they were going for the wrong reason. They ought to be there for GOD and to bring glory to His holy name.

"Are you doing the will of The Father?" Jackie would ask them.

He'd explain how if someone didn't know how to teach and preach, the thing leading up to that was to testify. He'd tell them that if they didn't know how to prophesy, the thing leading up to that was to encourage.

"GOD has a plan and a purpose for your life and I bind every spirit of fear that keeps any one of you bound and commit it to come out in Jesus' Name!" he'd say.

New people would come to the church, hearing about the special deliverance services that they'd have. Folks had told them that the miraculous would happen. People would be healed, renewed up in the Spirit, and even have devils cast out of them. It drew the desperate and the hurting alike. Unfortunately, it also brought out the crazies, odd, weirdos, and stranger folks – alongside the curious. And while some new people began coming there of the next few weeks, two more families would say goodbye and vow not to come back again for the reasoning that they didn't believe all of the things that were happening, even though they were happening right before their eyes – often to people who they'd known for years and otherwise trusted as genuine. One woman from the church had even verbally had it out with Pastor Jackie in the midst of all of this, screaming at him in shrill tones, in the foyer of the church, that she knew that she didn't have a demon – as though the rational default position would necessarily be to forbid someone to pray for you in a way that they hoped to work.

Quite frankly, Jackie felt as though if a man or woman of GOD prayed over someone someone with enough power to cast a devil out – and one wasn't there – a prayer of faith like that ought to have the power to heal them, anyhow. Throughout his ministry, his shepherd's heart had both been a blessing while at other times it seemed like a curse. As whole families who'd been a part of Souls Harbor Holiness Church for years extended their bitter goodbyes, the Nobles mourned their absence. He knew that Christ had suffered these things before and in vastly greater numbers. Entire towns would clear out to go hear this great teacher, healer, and alleged Messiah – then when He'd say something they didn't like or not be the image they'd imagined but rather the GOD who they could not begin to, they left the author of life and eventually consigned Him to death. Putting His Godhood aside, Jesus – even in his manhood – was a better man than Jackie. He was a better man than any who had ever been or would come thereafter. He was the Good Shepherd. This was one of the pronouncements that Christ had made. While Jackie was indeed a shepherd over one of the church's of GOD – none but GOD is truly good.

Jesus had made several declarations in regards to himself. He had said:

I AM – The Bread of Life (John 6)
I AM – The Light of the World (John 8)
I AM – The Gate of the Sheepfold (John 10)
I AM – The Good Shepherd (John 10)

I AM – The Resurrection and the Life (John 10)
I AM – The Way, the Truth, and the Life (John 14)
I AM – The True Vine (John 15)

Jackie could never be any one of these things. No mortal man could. The only characteristic of Christ that he could even aspire to put on that The LORD used in an "I AM" statement was when Jesus said – "I AM meek and lowly in heart." Thereby, day and night, as one who tended the fire of the altar in the house of GOD, Pastor Jackie would go hide himself away some place, get down on his knees in all humility, and praise the LORD of Heaven, who is mighty to save. It was during this time when he and his wife began receiving reports that Bishop Russell Ledbetter had publicly denounced him as a false teacher. In fact, from what they were hearing, there were a number of people within their organization who'd given ear to the slanderous backbiting against him – claiming that he was heretical. And while he was trying to do a mighty work for GOD, tension was building.

Phone calls would be coming in that he had to take and try to explain himself or even argue with someone who wanted to argue, but not listen to a thing that he said. Letters came in of all kinds and all sorts. Apparently, some of the churches around had taken issue with the things going on at Souls Harbor Holiness – and they let him know about it. Besides complaints, there were threats, though the threats were predominantly by phone. They'd range from hysterical screaming, cursing, or firing off one scripture after another, after another, after another, without taking a breath. Some of them would want to interrupt him while he was responding to them. Others would slam down the phone with such an intensity that the neighbors could probably just about hear the ding-sound from the Nobles' phone line to their homes. Very few contacts at that point had been from

the news media, even though the two of them that had been were told how he was on the docket to preach in Florida on Saturday evening, December 9th, 1972. His plan, thereby, was to have their very own Rev. Todd Driscoll cover for him that Sunday as he and Penny made the long drive back home.

Meanwhile, the phone would ring from around his breakfast time until after they'd gone to bed. During certain hours, Penny would take the phone off of the hook. It would be apologetically announced during service – along with individuals who people could call if something actually was an emergency – the hours that anyone should be able to get a call through, provided that the line wasn't tied up. In regards to how people saw things, he had quickly become one of the most talked-about pastors in the area. Howbeit, the fact of the matter was that Jackie Noble had never done any of this to be famous – he'd done it to be faithful, not that famous is even the right word. To many religious folks, the man whom they once regarded as their brother in Christ – all though some thinking him a peculiar sort for his Pentecostal heritage – had now been overshadowed by a sort of infamy. Like The LORD, he had a righteousness about him that drew sinners and the hurting, while the pious and self-righteous were left only with disdain.

Also like Christ, there were many who watched – as it were – from a distance. There they'd question whether or not this was real. They'd wonder, could it all be true? And while most certainly it was, a few odd fellows and actors had come into the church pretending like they had a demon and putting on a floorshow as a means of their overwhelming desire to be seen and show out. While they'd never admit that, of course, these were the same caliber of fools that fake speaking in tongues, fake dancing in the Spirit, and fake being slain in the

Spirit, which cause the weak-minded to doubt if these well-documented occurrences within the body of Christ are real at all. These were likened unto the testimonies of people who'd shout on Sunday and live like the world all week long. Perhaps, more tragic than the sacrilege of those who acted fools in this way, was the fact of the matter that there were amassments of people who couldn't tell the difference. Jackie, of course, sensed all of this madness – and he did the best that he could to keep an order to things. In his eyes, he thought of the whole affair being likened to the manager of a bank, who is being trained to spot counterfeit money. When the bank is doing that, they take the manager in training to where it is being printed. They have him look at the real money, hold the real money, and feel the real money extensively. It's just like that. When you've been around the real thing long enough – you'll know a fake when you see it.

Of the very many phone calls that he received, three of them were from his Pastor – the Rev. Dr. Byron Phillips. He'd notify him of the ugly nature that was shaping within their organization in regards to his casting out demons. It started in more of a gentle way, like a reproof, and progressively escalated into a fiery rebuke. Coming from this man, it hurt far worse than it would others. People of status within ministry were saying that Pastor Jackie Noble was heretical and false, so much that a part of him began to question whether he was. The pressure was enormous. It brought him to his knees, where time and time again, the Holy Spirit seemed to assure him that he was abiding in the perfect will of The Father, while these men who were called of GOD were being adversarial towards it.

Such were the innumerate and happenings concerning Rev. Jackie Noble between the time of his reinstatement as pastor at Souls Harbor Holiness Church and his speaking at the crusade in the state of Florida.

A Life
Well Lived

On the evening of Saturday, December 9th 1972, after a long leisurely drive that began early that morning, the Rev. Jackie Noble stood just off the main stage of a hall in Santa Rosa Beach, Florida, watching and listening to everything going on while concealed from the amassed crowd by some thick curtains between them. Before all of this, he had been greeted by the folks in charge. They were the very ones who'd contacted him and orchestrated this missional soul-saving and healing-type crusade. He patiently stood by in anticipation for the worship team to end their singing and playing, at which time the moderator would then call him up to the podium to preach. Deep down, a part of him began to think of how the song that the group was singing was actually a bit too contemporary for his liking. While he'd never heard it before, it could best be described as some sort of stoner-gospel. Several songs before that, the same band sang the Doobie Brothers' rock-'n'-roll song, "Jesus Is Just Alright with Me," which had been released to radio a month earlier – and while he didn't listen to secular music, he had heard it over the store radio at J. C. Penny – and raised an eyebrow thinking how they were performing a rock song, likely as a means to make themselves more relevant to any of the lost, worldly people there. It was a notion that struck him as odd. Did

Jesus Christ make himself more worldly, outside of coming to earth as a man, to draw the masses? The plain and simple truth was apparent. If ever there was a man who was Heavenly-minded, it was Jesus Christ. As his mind danced around all of this, the music continued to play.

Jackie did recognize that there was nothing necessarily sacrilegious about the lyrics and such of these songs. Still, the whole tone of their music just didn't sit right with him. He sincerely felt that music had just as much bearing on a song as the words. While they continued to play, he began to pray. He prayed through that song, getting all the more stirred up as he went. He continued to pray through the next song – by this point, relatively drowning it out all together. Thereafter, he prayed through the next and someone had to jostle him to tell the preacher that they were calling him up.

Approaching the podium, Jackie Noble held up his Bible, waving it at the people. He hugged the emcee's neck, took the microphone and began.

"Hallelujah! It's good to be here in the state of Florida. Your moderator and his wife both had a delightful conversation with me over the phone several weeks ago. They told me that like so many other people, they had read reports about my casting out devils, healing the sick, and saving the lost – and while that all sounds delightful and everything – I've never done a single one of those things, but Jesus has. The LORD saved my soul as a young boy, and I've been running on for him ever since. Let me tell you something: GOD has more for you that you could ever imagine. If you put your hope and trust in Him – if you make The LORD the desire of your heart – well, it'll be amazing what He'll do for you.

Ever since I was blessed with the opportunity to exorcize a drug-ridden teenager – who the world said had no hope – on an old dilapidated school bus, demoniacs have been coming out from behind every church pew and corner within a fifteen-foot radius of me, it seems. Friends, I've never got in a fight in my life that I didn't aim to win, and any devil that wants any part of me oughta know that the battle is the LORD's, the victory has been won, and anybody who gets too close to me with a devil inside them who wants to be free from it... Well, we're gonna make that devil homeless!"

With a thunderous response, Jackie Noble's declaration of war against the enemy unctioned those in attendance to clap and cheer enthusiastically. Thus, he continued. Systematically, he began to deconstruct the process of deliverance. He told them how if someone doesn't have Christ in their heart and a true intimacy with Him, then casting out a demon from that person – if possible – is unwise, for scripture tells us that it will come back with seven worse than itself and ravage their life far more terribly than before. There is no true freedom outside of a Christ-filled life. There are only temporal things that leave you dry and empty. Further, Jackie taught about renunciations – which is to say that GOD won't set you free from something that you don't really want to be set free from. The greatest of these, which too commonly gives the enemy a legal foothold to stay in a person's life, is unforgiveness.

"You don't forgive people for their sake. You forgive people for your sake. The Bible tells us that if we don't forgive, then we won't be forgiven. The

only way that you're going to be set free is by laying everything down at the cross and letting it go," he implored the congregation, adding how they needed to recognize the enemy, face the enemy, and do away with the enemy.

At another point in his message, Pastor Jackie thoughtfully explained that forgiving someone didn't mean keeping them around to abuse you. He told everyone there that they didn't need toxic people in their lives, nor did they need sympathetic connections. He spoke as to how a sympathetic connection is like a mangy dog on the side of the road that you pick up 'cause you feel sorry for it – and then you get the mange. From there he progressed into how there are a lot of things that as the followers of Jesus Christ that we – the Church – don't need to be connected to. Therein, he told of how life is filled with all kinds of things that we want to say don't affect us, shape us, or change us, but they do.

"Why, you could be around someone ugly. You'd know that they were ugly. You'd say that they were ugly, but after a while – they wouldn't seem so ugly anymore. Everything is just about like that. Your conscience gets seared to it. Nothing has changed but your perception – and its change is for the worse. This world is on its way to Hell and doesn't even know it. Is it any reason the Television calls them programs – when that's what they do? They call them channels 'cause they're casting a spell over you. They come from Hollywood – the type of wood that witches would make their wands from. The devil's name can be written all over something. He can make himself so plain, but when you cast your tent toward

Sodom, just like Lot, it doesn't look all that bad after too long," he said.

Within the construct of this sermon, Jackie spoke of the power of The Holy Ghost, the Authority of Jesus Christ – by whom alone men could be saved – deliverance, discipline, and sanctification. After that, he began to call people up to pray. First he gave an altar call, wherein some gave their hearts to The LORD, then he called for the sick and afflicted, as well as anyone who might have any sort of need to come up, so that he and the staff of prayer partners could pray with them. Thereafter, he told people if they were in bondage of any kind, he knew the chain-breaker. With other ministers, deacons, and intercessors gathered around, Jackie Noble began praying for people and casting devils out of them in Jesus' name – several of whom had multiple demonic entities inhabiting their persons. This all lasted for hours up into the night. There was crying; blood-curdling, tormented screaming; vomiting; people rolling around on the floor, contorting themselves. One woman slithered on the floor like a snake. Thereafter, Jackie and Penny – though exhausted – met up with the other leaders at a Denny's, where he got an omelet and some much-needed caffeine for the long road to their home in Georgia, that lay just ahead.

Amidst everything going on, Jackie didn't notice that there were several photographers taking photos for their respective newspapers and magazines there. Reporters were in attendance, as well as a man in the back with a video camera. One thing had led to another, and the people who wanted a story had just gotten one. They'd found a Holy Ghost-filled, tongue-talking, devil-stomping, water-baptized Preacher Man who was doing things just like Jesus did – and like the Apostle Paul delivering the Gospel with power and

authority – and thus another victory was won in the long-fought war against the enemy of the souls of mankind. While sprinkled throughout with the mighty works of GOD, Jackie Noble's life, like any Christian's, had a certain commonality and routine to it. While it is true that everyone for whom he'd ever prayed didn't get an immediate response or the thing that he'd hoped for, it is also true that one hundred percent of the people who never sought after a miracle or asked for prayer received nothing.

Sometimes it is not merely a matter of faith, nor the lack thereof. It is all a great mystery. In certain instances – such as with the man at the pool of Bethesda – Jesus Christ only came there to heal one particular person. Quite clearly, these other people had faith and were gathered about for what later texts – which were translated into the King James Bible – would call an angel stirring the waters. Yet, Christ only did what He did and because of who He is we know that He did it perfectly. Jackie Noble, like each of us, only looked through life like a veil darkly, with things being obscured to him until the day that he went home to be with The LORD. His life was not about casting out demons, but rather, following after Jesus Christ from day to day in a life that brought glory to the Heavenly Father. All else was just a byproduct of the life that he lived.

Certainly, more people would be drawn to his ministry and have great confidence in him due to the miraculous signs and wonders that were evident in it. All the while, more detractors would arise to wage war with him inside the walls of his church and the organization to which he'd belonged. Due to this, he'd eventually leave his beloved state of Georgia to pastor elsewhere as The LORD provided, likewise transferring from one J. C. Penny department store to another. Besides all of this, things would grow ever more distant between him and Dr. Byron Phillips. The man – whom he once regarded as a pastor, a friend, and the mantle over him – would become little more than a shadow of the past. On one of their last occasions together – feeling strongly to pray over the elder pastor's wife – Joyce, who sat bound in her wheelchair, sometimes pleading for her husband to let him see her and pray over her and other times cursing him, as if there were two different beings talking out of her – Dr. Phillips refused to allow it. Their final goodbye left them with him calling Jackie a freak. As he walked away for the final time, shaking the dust from his feet, something deep within him mourned Sister Joyce Phillips. He could feel her watching – and perhaps something else.

Joyce's mouth curled into a smile as her hope for freedom walked out that door – continuing on the way called straight. Like a whisper, unreasonable laughter flowed out of her. The gross abuse that she had suffered had opened her up to such terrors as many will never know. Broken and afflicted, she lived under the care of her husband and his dull-witted paramour until the day that she died in her own bed. They found her there, and yet her smile wasn't one of malignancy as is sometimes seemed during her laughing spells, nor was there any sorrow in her face as there often was at other times. Instead, she had the sweet look of peace as though she had seen the angels in the room with her as the silver cord was rent and they whisked her off unto a better land.

Dr. Byron would thereafter move his mistress from out of his home and put distance between the two of them, to later marry again, and leave his second wife a widow. Many would forget the stories of the miraculous that were written in the newspapers, magazines, told on radio and television of the small-town Georgia Holiness Pastor, who did mighty things in the name of Jesus Christ – and yet there is a record in Heaven of all those who are faithful. In the years to come, Jackie and Penny Noble would adopt a child who'd been cast away. Penny had always wanted to be a mother and Jackie a dad. In this, it seemed that The LORD too had made a way.

About the Author
B.L. BLANKENSHIP

Born in 1981 from the fires of revivalistic prayer meetings, ceaseless fasting, and believing, Rev. Benjamin Lee Blankenship was conceived by two Southern parents – his mother (Jonelle), a Church of God woman from Harlan, Kentucky; and his father (Larry), a Jesus'-name baptized Apostolic from Pulaski, Tennessee, whom the doctors had said would be incapable of having any other children due to his father having a vasectomy for so long. For over a year, Jonelle had prayed with intensity, beseeching The LORD for a baby boy and pledging to give him over to GOD – like Hannah in the Old Testament did with her son, the prophet Samuel. She stood in one prayer line after another, being prayed for by Dr. T. L. Lowery, Pastor Tony Scott, and other less widely known ministers. From a young age, he had an interest in music, ministry, and art. All of these were placed in him by The LORD and cultivated into what became his professional career as a graphic artist, a lyricist, drummer, music producer, singer, and minister of the Gospel of Jesus Christ.

Directed by the Holy Ghost to preach at the age of seven, Benjamin ran and hid from his calling until finally professing it at fourteen. He preached his first sermon on Wednesday, April 21st, 1999; began his first of three nursing-home ministries on Friday, October 13th, 2000; pastored his first church from ages twenty to twenty-one; and evangelized primarily across Tennessee, Kentucky, Alabama, Georgia, Ohio, Missouri, and West Virginia. During his pastorate of Benchmark Church (circa JAN. 2015- JUL. 2022), he began writing both non-fiction and fiction as an emotional release as well as an added stream of revenue. Notably, his nonfiction and fiction stand in complete contrast one from another. 100% of the nonfiction is reflective of the theological/ministerial and/or about leadership. Meanwhile, his fiction under B. L. Blankenship is predominantly (#1) within the most extreme fringe of graphically violent horror, and (#2) set within the late 19th Century. Jodie Walls Rides Again [originally titled Josey Wales Rides Again, but changed due to copyright] is his only traditional Western/coming-of-age novel that is suitable for children. It contains a lot of cigarette smoking, and later gun violence, with the most disparaging scene being when a foul teenager brutally kills Jodie Walls' small Shih Tzu dog, a crime subsequently leading to the outlaw shooting him to death and burying him – like trash – in an unmarked grave. The three-volume serial, Abraham Lincoln Burns in Hell, is written like a collection of journal entries, newspaper clippings, and whatnot from and concerning the interdimensional traveler, John Wilkes Booth, who has been tasked with the mission of assassinating tyrannical variants of Abraham Lincoln on alternate versions of Earth – and while complexly nuanced, might otherwise be regarded as family friendly. Finally, Chronicles of the Velveteen Preacher: The Dark City & World of Sin contains three of the many short stories that were written nearly a decade before B. L. Blankenship's authorship began (circa 2019).

Details from B. L. Blankenship's former aspirations of being in law enforcement, his extensive studies within theology, demonology, and history are all quite apparent throughout his fiction. His complete bibliography up unto the point of this book's publication is as follows:

––––––––––––– NOVELS –––––––––––––

God Walks the Dark Hills

BOOKS I–VI

The vast majority of songs and musical works ascribed to the author can be found in relation to his decommissioned band/group name, by which he has also been widely know within the world of Southern Gospel Music – BEN*JAM. His music also includes, Praise and Worship, Christian Rock, Christian Rap, Bluegrass Gospel, Barbershop Quartet Gospel, etc. Both at the non-fiction author Benjamin Blankenship and event more so the fiction author B. L. Blankenship, his literature is widespread.

Thank you for reading the novel:
Holy Ghost Exorcist

Milton Keynes UK
Ingram Content Group UK Ltd.
UKHW020922181223
434584UK00001BA/219